By the same author

Historical Fiction

The Hanging Tree
Where Seagulls Fly (2013 Edition)
Song of the Sea
The Shepherd of St Just

Selected Other Fiction

The Black Rose (short stories)
Eve White
For Love or Money
The Magical Isles Trilogy (Compendium Edition)
Quiddity
The Red Brick Road
Synergy

Mind Body Spirit

The Empty Cup
Enlightenment: One Man's Search for the Truth of Existence
Everyday Magic
Intuition: A User's Guide
Reality Perception
There is Only Now

Runaway

By Edwin Page

Curved Brick

First published to Kindle & paperback in 2016
by Curved Brick, UK

No.64

To those who know that freedom is a state of body *and* mind

1

He was robed in the darkness of a moonless night as he crouched in the bushes, damp with sweat and trembling. His arms and face stung with the abrasions of his flight through the brush. The hounds were close, their eager cries rising into the stillness to mingle with the calls of the farmhands in pursuit.

Joshua shifted with discomfort, his grubby vest clinging to his body and irritating the fresh lashes upon his back. The pain of the wounds had sent him into the night with the conviction to be free and served to spur him on with greater force than the baying of the dogs.

He peered from his concealment with wide eyes as his heart pounded. The sky in the east was paling, the leaves and branches of the bushes silhouetted against the waning shadow of the small hours.

Lanterns moved within a stretch of woodland to his left, like fireflies caught behind the black bars of the tree trunks. Vague shapes of men could be seen carrying them as they searched shrub and thicket, the beating of sticks mingling with the other sounds of the hunt.

Breaking cover, Joshua stayed low and moved away in the opposite direction. Grasses sighed against his britches and the dew gathered upon their blades washed against his bare feet as he passed.

Quail broke the hush of the grassland with urgent fluttering and cries of alarm as they flew from thick undergrowth ahead of him. Startled, Joshua veered towards a dark strand of trees to the west, the sky above still adorned with the stars of night's retreating robe.

The dogs bayed with renewed vigour and he knew his scent had been rediscovered. He gritted his teeth and forced himself onward, legs aching and body weary after hours of fleeing the harsh life he had known upon the farm.

Entering the trees, one of his braces snagged on a branch as it hung loose at his side, the supports too painful against his wounds to be worn over his shoulders. The leaves rustled in agitation and a twig snapped as he pulled it free, the sound making him wince.

Joshua moved between the trunks, stumbling over a fallen timber. Sweat dripped into his eyes and he wiped it away with the back of his hand, blinking to clear his vision. He tried to make his way with stealth, but his weakening legs carried great weight and progress was laboured.

The hounds were closing. If the paleness of his vest was seen moving through the darkness, the handlers would release their charges. The final chapter of his bid for freedom would be brought to an end in the rapid approach of fervent panting followed by bloodied screams. If he were lucky, he'd be killed. If not, he would be taken back and further punishment would be metered out.

Pushing through a thicket of undergrowth, he fell into a creek which had been hidden beyond, its presence a black ribbon passing through the landscape. Unable to swim, he flailed in the water, head temporarily ducking beneath the surface as he turned and tried to reach for the bank.

Grasping the bowed heads of bank-side grasses, he attempted to pull himself free. His stamina all but exhausted, his hold on the meagre blades slipped loose and he was carried downstream by the firm current that was swollen by recent rains.

Joshua struggled, his head dipping under for ever longer periods and his movements becoming more frantic as he fought to find breath. He resurfaced, gasping and spluttering, spitting water and feeling all strength fading from him limbs.

His right hand briefly touched upon something solid amidst the disturbance. He blinked water from his eyes and saw the indistinct shape of a log.

Desperately reaching for it with both hands, Joshua drew it to his breastbone, the wood rotting and soft beneath his clutching fingers. He wrapped his arms about its presence as they were steadily taken south by the waters. His body trailing like a withered and battered limb, he breathed deeply and closed his eyes, the cries of the hounds receding as he sank into unconsciousness.

Clara sat cross-legged upon the ground, a scattering of straw about her. She cradled the doc against her chest, the rabbit seeming large against her diminutive form. Humming a gentle tune, she petted it as the birds sung in the trees outside the barn and daybreak brought the first beams of sunlight slanting between the slats in the wall above the hutches.

'Clara!'

She looked to the doors. 'I be a coming,' she responded to her mother's call.

'It be time for you to go back now, Elsa,' she said softly to the rabbit, bending to kiss its head before awkwardly rising.

Clara stepped to the two lines of hutches against the eastern wall of the barn, some on the floor and others upon a shelf above. Motes of dust marked her disturbance and glimmered in the sunbeams as she opened the top-right cage and carefully placed Elsa onto the straw inside before fastening the door.

'I'll bring you a treat later,' she stated, peering into the hutch and briefly putting her hand to the wire at the front, waggling a finger in farewell.

She turned and made her way to the doors, bare feet padding on the compacted earth as she glanced at the other rabbits within their confinement. 'I'll be bringing you all a treat,' she announced brightly.

Clara exited the barn and brushed stray pieces of straw from her pale green dress, the hem just below her knees.

She walked across the path that ran to the east fields and entered the fenced chicken run. Stepping to the coop, she slid the low hatch open, hearing one of the creatures murmur within.

Making her way back out of the high gate, she walked alongside South Field, breathing deeply to draw in the scent of the ripening corn that was heavy in the cool morning air. She glanced at the axe rising between her and the low boundary fence as she approached the cottage, the head of the implement buried in the scarred surface of the chopping block.

Stepping onto the front porch, she checked for any further signs of her visit to the barn and then entered. Her mother turned from the stove on the opposite side of the room, wearing loose fitting overalls with a grey blouse beneath. Her light brown hair was tied back as usual, but a few coiled and thin strands remained to the sides of her face.

'Did you be taking yourself to the barn?' asked Lizbet as she regarded her daughter.

Clara turned her gaze to the floorboards and made her way over to the table that dominated the right-hand side of the main room. 'I only went to visit with Elsa,' she responded as she took a seat.

'What have I done told you about giving them names?' She frowned, noting a piece of straw caught in her daughter's long dark hair.

She stepped over and plucked it from the wild waves which tumbled down Clara's back. 'It'll only lead to tears,' she stated in a softer tone. 'They're for food, fur and bartering, so it be best you not be getting attached.'

'I know,' responded the girl, placing a hand on the tabletop and tracing a knot in the wood with her fingernail, 'but we've so many, be there need to kill them all?' She looked up, her brown eyes pleading.

'In time,' nodded Lizbet.

'Even Elsa?'

'We'll see,' she conceded, moving back to the stove and stirring the broth simmering in the large cooking pot.

'She be a good breeder,' insisted Clara. 'Pa done told me we need to keep the breeding stock.'

'I said, we'll see,' replied Lizbet.

She poured the contents of the pot into dinted metal bowls resting on the cabinet beside her and then took them to the table. The bread board and spoons had already been placed, Clara taking hers up as one of the bowls was set before her. Lizbet seated herself to the left of her daughter, the light spilling in through the open shutters opposite her chasing the shadows from the hollows of her thin face.

Lizbet looked over and raised her eyebrow meaningfully as she placed her palms together in readiness for prayer. Sagging, Clara lowered the spoon back to the tabletop and followed suit.

'For what we are about to receive, may the Good Lord make us thankful,' said Lizbet, temporarily closing her eyes.

'Amen,' they said together.

Clara took up her spoon again as the steam of the vegetable broth wafted into her face. She dipped it into the thin soup, a piece of potato drawn onto it with the liquid. Raising it to her mouth, she blew on the surface, watching the ripples before supping tentatively and finding the heat bearable.

Lizbet reached forward and drew the bread board towards her, cutting a thick slice and looking to her daughter, who nodded in response. She cut another and passed it over, a few crumbs falling to the tabletop.

Clara ripped the tough bread, seeing spots of mould upon the crust. She used the pieces to wipe up the last of

6

the meagre sustenance, running them around the edge of the bowl and finding that the staleness was not masked by the tastelessness of the broth.

'You're to take the bowls and pot to The Eddy and then set to sweeping the floors,' stated Lizbet as she fetched two tin cups and a jug of water, pouring some into each.

'When you're done, we have need to gather more firewood,' she added, passing a cup to her daughter.

Clara nodded and raised it to her mouth, taking a drink and wiping her lips with the back of her hand. She looked to the seat opposite her, the empty chair with its back to the large stone-built chimney that dominated the western end of the main room. 'It may be that Pa will return home today,' she commented, turning to her mother.

Lizbet's gaze flitted to where her husband had once sat at the table before turning to the water remaining in her cup. She stared at the play of light upon its surface. 'It may be,' she nodded, her gaze thoughtful as she briefly scratched her long thin nose, her daughter's more rounded and lips fuller, both attributes inherited from her father.

Clara reached down, a grimace upon her face as she scratched her ankle, her shoulder nudging the table and causing it to wobble. Lizbet watched, thinking of making comment as she cradled her cup of water, elbows upon the tabletop. Her daughter's skin was susceptible to irritation by hay and straw, and her visit to the barn had clearly caused a reaction.

Deciding to hold her tongue, she finished the last of her water. Crows called noisily overhead, their cries echoing down the chimney stack as she thought about Walter, recalling the day he'd left for the war. He'd sat proud upon his horse, smiling in the fall sunshine, his bed roll slung over his back and rifle holstered.

They'd shared a last kiss, Walter leaning down as she stood on tiptoes, their lips barely touching. Without a word, he'd turned Rosco and made his way along the track that led from the cottage, passing along the side of South Field. The light morning mist was touched with the warm light of a new day, softening the fresh furrows made by the plough and the trees beyond. It was a scene that returned to her again and again, his vague figure moving away within the diffused landscape like a receding dream onto which she longed to cling.

Lizbet sighed and set her cup down. She arose from her seat, the scrape of its legs against the floorboards accompanying her movement.

'Should I be feeding the rabbits before going to The Eddy?' asked Clara as she sat up straight, the skin about her ankle reddened by her scratching.

'They can wait,' replied Lizbet. 'Now, take yourself to the crick. There are plenty of chores need doing and the day is past waking.'

Clara reached down and began to scratch again.

Lizbet stepped over as her daughter straightened. 'Leave the irritation be and find some haste in those legs of yours,' she said, putting her hand to the side of the girl's head and giving it a gentle push.

Clara rose without enthusiasm and emptied the remaining water in her cup back into the jug. Placing the empty vessel into her bowl, she piled them on her mother's and then placed all in the cooking pot. Leaving the items on the cabinet by the stove, she went to the doorway leading to the hall opposite the entrance to the cottage.

'Where might you be going?'

'To fetch Rosie,' answered Clara over her shoulder as she moved down the hall and went to the second door on the right. 'She can be helping with the dishes.'

She entered her room. It was a small enclosure that had been part of the food store before she came of age to require her own room, the odours of earth and potatoes still rising from the floorboards when dampness set in. There was space enough for a bed along the right-hand wall and rough shelving in the corner by the small rearward window, but no more.

Clara stepped to the cot and picked up the doll resting on her hay-filled pillow. Holding it, she stroked its deep red hair of twisted wool and smiled fondly. Its head and body were made of pale cloth, her mother having created happy eyes and a smile of black stitching. Its blue dress had been fashioned from one of her father's flannel shirts and he had stuffed the doll using further cuttings from the tatty piece of clothing, her parents having combined their efforts to create the Christmas gift two winters previous.

'We be going to the crick,' she informed the doll before tucking it into the cord tied around her waist and heading back to the main room.

Taking up a stained piece of cloth from the cabinet, she draped it over her shoulder and lifted the pot laden with dirty dishes. She walked to the front door and opened it, glancing at the pair of lounging chairs and stool resting on the other side of the room from the table. A faded rug lay between and there was an old dresser beyond. A grandmother clock that had been passed down her mother's line stood silent against the back wall, time stilled upon its pale face.

Pausing, she turned to her mother, blinking away the image of her parents seated in the chairs. 'What are you to do while I visit the crick?'

Lizbet frowned and looked at her daughter meaningfully. 'It be best that you're away to The Eddy. Mr Tyler is in want of six pelts and we are in need of meat.'

Clara's pulse became elevated. 'Not Elsa?' she asked nervously.

Her mother shook her head. 'Not Elsa,' she confirmed.

Swallowing back, she still felt sickened by the thought of what her mother must do while she abided at the creek. She felt a little relief that her favoured doe would remain unharmed, but pitied those that'd find their lives brought to an end in a twist and snap.

Clara hesitated a moment before stepping out onto the porch. Her mother watched the door close behind the girl and shook her head. She worried for her daughter. A seam of gentleness ran through her nature, deep and wide. It was beyond the mere innocence of youth and showed no sign of being mined by experience. Such gentleness was ill suited to the life they lived, was a hindrance that made her weak in a harsh world.

Lizbet sighed. 'Her sweetness could be her undoing,' she mumbled as she thought about the prospect of Walter failing to return from the war and some chance mishap befalling her, leaving Clara alone and all but helpless.

Shaking her head again, she chided herself for such bleak thoughts. 'He will return,' she stated, feeling the doubt that lurked within like some villain hiding in the shadows.

3

Joshua felt the warmth of the sun upon his cheek. His eyes closed, the presence of his body crept into awareness. The ache of muscles pushed through the lingering lethargy of the weariness that had overcome him. His existence was dull pain.

Cool dampness pressed against the left side of his face and he felt pressure upon his eye. His legs felt weightless and his brow creased as he tried to fathom the cause of the sensation.

The ripple of water washed into Joshua's mind and muddied thoughts of splashing and encapsulation moved into his consciousness, contained in darkness and touched with fear. He recalled the creek as he attempted to move his legs and grimaced with discomfort. Ripples of disturbance followed and he felt the wetness of his britches.

Moving his head to relieve the pressure on his eye, he prepared to leave the dark womb in which he was held. His lids rose and he looked out through narrow slits, his existence expanding like an exhalation as he discovered the world beyond his individual nature. There was mud before his face and a bed of reeds beyond, still and silent.

Straining to look down his body, his sight was filled with flashes of brightness and he winced. Sunlight danced on the waters of the creek, its meander stretching away into the distance.

His arm was draped over something hard and he turned his gaze to the timber nestled against his side. Memories stirred. He heard the baying of dogs, felt the sting of branches against his skin. The lash of a whip drew up from the depths. His wrists were bound to the whipping post, back bare. Willard Ford was smiling as he drew the length of leather through his hand, caressing it as he savoured the sensation of power. Other slaves watched as Joshua pleaded his innocence, the large farmhand ignoring all protests.

Twenty lashes followed in the snap of leather on skin. He gritted his teeth, jaw clenched tight as he tried not to cry out, but yells of pain were forced from his lips by the strength of the final strikes.

He lay on the bank and felt the wounds upon his back. The vest was stuck to them and there was an itching which grew as his mind turned to their presence.

Joshua closed his eyes, finding no strength to rise or to continue exploring his condition. His body sank against the mud, the tension lifting away.

All was darkness. He was immersed in water, struggling in desperation. It splashed into his eyes and up his nose as he fought to keep his head above the surface, his body like a lead weight dragging him down.

Mouth tightly shut and lungs straining, he was drawn into the crushing black with his eyes fixed upon a pale and distant light above. It was stained red and sang to him with the voice of a child, the words unintelligible through the thickness of the water.

Lungs fit to burst, he opened his mouth and released his last breath, the water rushing into the vacancy.

Joshua's eyes snapped open and then narrowed against the glare of the day. Confusion followed in wake of the dream, his mind temporarily befuddled. The sound of a girl singing wound through the confusion and he thought it a remnant of the sleep borne vision.

The girl's voice grew steadily louder and the words became distinct.

'Rosie, oh Rosie, you're my best friend,
Pull a stitch and I will mend,
As sweet as molasses, as warm as the sun,
At my side when day is done.'

The verse came to an end, the melody of her voice absorbed by his mind as the girl continued with the next.

'Rosie, oh Rosie, you're my best friend,
Side by side 'til the very end.
A Missouruh smile upon your face,
A belle of the south, make no mistake.'

Joshua looked for a place to hide as the girl began to repeat the song. He tried to rise, but there was little strength by which to do so.

The voice drew ever closer. An idea came to mind and he backed himself into the creek, face taut with pain and as he used the bank to drag his floating body to the concealment of the reed bed.

He drew into the shadows, head pulsing and muscles aching. Staring out, he watched as a young girl with a wilderness of long dark hair approached from the right. She passed onto the mud flats and crouched near the log which had saved him the previous night.

Setting the cooking pot down, Clara lifted out the other items and rested them on the bank. She took Rosie from beneath the cord about her waist and seated the doll against the log beside her.

'You can be enjoying the sun,' she said with a smile before taking up the pot and leaning forward.

Clara went still, the pot held just above the surface. She stared at the muddied water by the bank and her brow furrowed.

She looked out over the bend in the creek, its course changing from south to west. The waters had worn away the near bank during countless fall rains and spring thaws, creating a pool of sorts. Her mother referred to it as The Eddy, but her father had called it The Rump when Lizbet was out of earshot.

Seeing only flotsam on the eddying current near her position, she turned her gaze to the vague stain of mud on the far bank which indicated how far the level had dropped during the summer. The creak of timber briefly took her attention to the strand of trees beyond, some of their roots arcing over the waters and vanishing into their depths.

Seeing nothing untoward, Clara shrugged. 'Must've been a startled fish, ain't that right, Rosie?' she asked the doll, pausing a moment as if listening to a response before lowering the pot into the water and using her fingers to wash it out.

The strain of its weight evident upon her face, she lifted the pot with both hands and poured out the water. She took the cloth from her shoulder and proceeded to dry the vessel. Setting it upon the step of drier ground to her left when she was satisfied, she turned to Rosie.

'One down,' she commented, taking up a bowl and dipping it in the creek.

Joshua watched as the girl cleaned bowls, cups and spoons. She spoke at regular intervals to the doll seated with its back to the log and was completely unaware of his presence amidst the reeds. He tried to keep his breathing steady, the throbbing of his head causing his sight to blur from time to time as he stared out from his hiding place.

It wasn't long until each item had been placed washed and cleaned into the cooking pot, the damp cloth draped over the top. The girl rested back on her haunches and looked north up the creek, the reflection of sunlight upon the ripples playing across her face as she took up a twig and idly stuck it into the mud at the water's edge.

'I don't want to be going back yet,' she stated to the doll with a sideways glance. 'Ma will be skinning them by now.' She flicked a piece of dry mud into the water and watched the ripples widen.

Joshua watched as they gently washed against the stems of the outlying reeds. Every moment the girl lingered increased the chances of discovery and his discomfort within the creek grew.

He felt something wriggle past his ankle and fought against the urge to withdraw his foot. The girl talked to her doll again, lifting it from the ground and setting it upon her lap.

'We'd better be making our way back or Ma will come looking for us,' she stated regretfully as she stroked the doll's red hair and then flattened creases out of its dress. 'At least I'll have done missed the worst of it.'

Seeing movement in the periphery of her vision, Clara looked up. The curled fingers of scum that rested upon the surface of The Eddy were undulating in the wake of agitation.

'A fish, judging from the pattern,' she said to the doll as lines of ripples widened and faded.

She watched a while longer, hearing the call of a heron upstream. Tucking Rosie back into the cord, she picked up the pot with both hands and stood.

Making her way onto the step of drier ground, she began towards the boundary fence. She looked to the house, expression tightening as she thought of the scene which would greet her upon entry.

Joshua watched her leave and listened to the pad of her feet receding from the creek when she'd passed from sight. The sound of a gate opening and closing followed shortly after and he slumped against the bank, the reeds about him sighing as if echoing his relief.

4

Clara stepped onto the porch and hesitated. She looked longingly down the hallway opposite the open front door, wishing she could pass through the main room without pause so as to avoid the grizzly sight of her mother's progress with the rabbits.

'You done took more time than a Tennessee mule,' commented Lizbet as she stepped into view.

Clara walked into the house, glancing at the furs in the stretcher frames upon the table. 'I saw a fish,' she commented, her stomach light.

'Ain't nothing unusual in that,' responded Lizbet. 'Now, come and help me with the meat.'

Clara looked to her in alarm, the carcasses on the counter beside the stove haunting the edge of her vision. 'I thought I was to sweep the floors,' she replied, noting the salt stuck to her mother's palms.

'The sweeping can wait.' Lizbet went over to the skinned rabbits, two already rubbed with salt and placed to the side. 'One day you'll be needing to do this without my help, so it be best you learn now.' She put her hands to one of the bodies and began to rub the flesh with vigour.

'I can't,' moaned Clara, sickened by both the sight of her mother's activities and the thought of doing the same.

'You can and you will. Put down the pot and come here,' said Lizbet over her shoulder.

Clara hesitated. She was unwilling to participate, but also to disobey her mother, the resulting struggle keeping her in place, her expression showing her plight.

'Stop dawdling and do as I say.' Lizbet gave her daughter a stern look, feeling guilty at having foisted such a task upon her, but knowing that she must toughen if she was to thrive.

Clara forced herself to the table and pulled out a chair, using her foot about one of the front legs to do so. She placed the cooking pot upon its surface, the tightness of her shoulders after carrying the load from the creek adding to her feeling of tension. She hesitated again, gaze on the furs pulled tight as they dried in the simple wooden frames on the tabletop.

'I won't be telling you again.'

She walked over to her mother's side with stuttering steps. Looking to the carcasses, her stomach churned, the smell of the meat serving to heighten the nausea.

'I feel sick,' she stated.

'It'll pass,' said her mother turning. 'Cover your hands in salt,' she instructed, glancing to the bowl on the countertop.

Feeling close to tears, Clara raised her hands and placed them palm down in the wide bowl. The damp salt clung to her skin. She held them out before her and stared at the coating, swallowing hard as she thought of what she must do next.

'Step up,' said Lizbet, moving over a little and placing one of the remaining rabbits at her daughter's intended position.

Clara stared at it with wide eyes. Her heart pounded and her stomach churned as she moved to stand directly before it, her hands raised and trembling.

'I just can't,' she said, shaking her head as the first tears rolled down her cheeks.

She bolted from the room, Rosie slipping from the cord and falling to the floorboards.

'Clara!' Lizbet called after her, hearing her daughter pass down the hall and into her bedroom.

Sobbing could be heard to the rear of the cottage and Lizbet sighed, her hands to the meat she'd been salting. Her anxiety about her daughter's ability to survive mingled with the ache she felt at the sounds of Clara's distress.

Finishing the task, she stepped out onto the porch and dusted the salt from her palms as she looked out over the field of corn in front of the house. The sun bathed the ripening heads in warmth as they stirred in a gentle breeze and grasshoppers sounded within the grasses by the boundary fence to the left of the house.

Turning to go back into the cottage, her gaze settled on a curl of dark hair caught in the grass by the porch. She went still, eyes temporarily glazing over as she recalled trimming Walter's beard the evening before he left for the war, one of the dining chairs having been removed to the porch.

She'd stood before him and taken her time, the task a ritual of farewell as she tried to commit every contour of his rugged face to memory. When she'd finished they'd looked into each other's eyes for long moments before he'd risen and gone inside to say goodnight to Clara, his intention to leave before she'd risen the following morning.

Frowning and feeling a pang of loneliness, Lizbet turned back and went into the shadows. Taking up the rabbits by the cords that bound their back legs, she took them along the hall to the pantry. The sound of her daughter's distress arose from the room next door, tugging at her heartstrings as she hung the carcasses from the ceiling, sacks of vegetables against the wall on the left and shelves sparsely laden with preserves opposite, the store heavy with the scent of earth.

Shutting the door, she turned and stepped back into the main room, looking down at Rosie as her daughter's sobs began to die away. She took up the doll, looking at her smiling face and briefly neatening her hair.

'What am I to do?' she asked softly.

No answer was forthcoming.

Continuing to hold the doll before her, Lizbet passed back into the hallway, stopping before the door to her daughter's room near its end. Bolstering herself with a breath, she knocked.

'Clara?' she enquired as she entered.

Her daughter was curled upon her cot, legs hugged to her chest and eyes raw as she looked up.

Lizbet stepped over and seated herself on the edge of the bed. 'Here,' she said, holding Rosie towards her.

Clara reached out and took the doll, taking it to her breast in a tight grip, her fingers still touched with salt.

'I'm sorry,' said Lizbet softly, brushing hair from her daughter's forehead, 'but it be for your own good. I fret over what will become of you if I succumb to some illness or injury.'

'I know,' responded Clara weakly, 'but I just couldn't.'

Lizbet nodded as she withdrew her hand. 'There's still sweeping to be done, unless you'd prefer to be taking the washboard to the crick?'

'I'll sweep,' said Clara, wiping her nose with the back of her hand. 'Then I'll come to The Eddy and help with the washing,' she added.

Lizbet smiled thinly and nodded. 'Your company would be welcome. There be both linen and clothing to be cleaned today.'

She looked at her daughter's forlorn expression and felt the ache in her chest. Rising, she went to the door, holding its edge and turning. 'We'll try again when you feel ready.'

Clara nodded and sniffed.

Lizbet hesitated as her daughter slowly sat up. Exiting, she passed along the hall, turning her gaze to the brightness beyond the open front door and seeing a blue jay sweep past on its way to the creek.

'A sign of change to come,' she said to herself, remembering what her mother had said in reference to the birds as she went to the buckets resting on the floor beside the cabinet.

She took up the nearest, a small washboard leaning within. Turning, her gaze went to the stretched skins upon the table.

'May it be a change for the good,' she mumbled, the nagging concerns about her daughter's soft nature giving rise to a worried frown.

5

Joshua moved from the reeds, staying close to the bank. Slowly standing, his legs still feeling weak, he peered over the grasses to the cottage beyond.

Seeing no sign of activity, he dragged himself out of the creek as quietly as he could, keeping a wary eye on the farmstead. He unsteadily moved to the side of the building, tucking himself beside the wide chimney breast and leaning against the slats of the wall.

Weeping emanated from within and he glanced over his shoulder, sure that it arose from the girl that had visited the creek. Gathering his reserves of strength, he moved to the rear corner and stepped over the low boundary fence, nearly loosing his balance as he did so.

Passing along the rear of the house, Joshua kept low, his progress slow and teeth gritted against the pain in his back. He came to a halt by a small window, the shutters open on the day. Crying spilled out as he moved beneath the sill, resisting the temptation to raise himself in order to see the cause of the upset.

A knock sounded from within. He stiffened and paused just beyond the window, listening for what may follow.

'Clara?' It was a woman's voice that issued from the room.

The vague sounds of softly spoken words followed him as Joshua continued along the rear wall. He reached the corner of the cottage, his legs made tremulous by his exertions. A modest barn lie ahead, trees beyond and to its rear. A goat was tethered in the grass between the buildings and a clothes line hung across the ten yard gap.

Making his way with as much haste as he could muster, Joshua crossed a well-worn path that let to an outhouse nestled in front of the trees to his right. He went to the side of the barn, perspiration building upon his face and feeling faint.

He hesitantly put his eye to a hole in the wood and peered into the gloom, having to blink bleariness from his vision. Rabbit hutches rested opposite his vantage point and there were two stalls to the left with a hayloft above. A horned cow rested in the nearside stall, the other empty and looking disused, its floor clear of straw and a few dusty cobwebs hanging from the timbers.

Joshua took a few breaths, the pain of his wounds causing him to grimace as he moved towards the front of the building, his hand to the slats for support. He checked that there was still no sign of anyone about the cottage, eyes narrowed against the brightness of the cornfield and head pounding.

Seeing no one, he moved to the doors. He glanced at a pair of chickens pecking and scraping in the run on the other side of the path and then slipped into the building.

He paused, leaning against the wall beside the doors and wiping his forehead with the back of his hand. One of the rabbits scrabbled within its cage, the sound filling the hush of the interior as his head swam with momentary dizziness.

Pushing off from the slats with a grunt of effort once the sensation had passed, he made his way beyond the hutches to the ladder that led to the hayloft. Taking hold of the sides, he slowly willed himself to the top, longing for rest. Each step took tremendous effort, his legs threatening to buckle at any moment and his entire body complaining as sweat dripped down his face.

Joshua reached the top and kept his head low beneath the eaves, the last of his stamina all but spent. He sought out the deepest shadows and moved to the rear left, stumbling in the straw.

Collapsing in the corner, he rested on his back and covered himself as best he could. The rich and musty scent of the straw filled him and drew him down into sleep, his eyes closing as he succumbed willingly and crows called in the trees outside.

6

Clara's lids snapped open, the squeals of terror and bulging eyes replaced by the blackness of her room. Her heart raced as she lay upon her cot, the cries of rabbits receding into the depths of her mind. She could feel the night air against her left leg and felt for the cover, finding it in disarray and draped over the side.

Fumbling in the pitch, she pulled it back over herself, feeling the soreness of her fingertips after using the washboard the previous day. She looked to the shutters, head heavy upon the pillow. The faintest light could be seen through the gap between, night holding sway as day took its waking breath and prepared to exhale.

Closing her eyes, Clara tried to settle and find sleep, the echoes of the dream having faded to a distant whisper in the corridors of her mind. She lay on her back for a while but soon found herself turning onto her side, feeling something brushing against her nose beyond the edge of the pillow.

She reached out and her fingers closed about Rosie. Smiling, she drew the doll beneath the covers and held her close.

Sleep would not come and she rolled onto her other side, the wall only inches from her face in the deep gloom. Birds began to call in the trees behind the buildings as they awoke, their songs as yet subdued by the weight of the darkness that was slowly being chased from the east.

Clara sat up, the cover falling away and the chill touch of the morning air causing her bare arms to tingle. Continuing to hold Rosie, she slipped her legs out over the side and pulled the coarse bed sheet from her lap. She stood and then padded to the door in her pale nightgown, opening it with care.

She stepped into the hallway and felt a slight tug on the doll clasped in her left hand. It was accompanied by the brief sound of tearing and she lifted Rosie to inspect her as she set off towards the main room, having to concentrate her gaze due to the scant illumination. A few stitches had been pulled apart at the back of her dress and Clara glanced over her shoulder, certain a splinter in the doorframe had snagged the blue flannel.

'Son of a bitch,' she whispered as she walked into the main room.

'Clara!'

She jumped and turned her gaze to the indistinct figure of her mother as she came to a halt. Lizbet was seated at the table, the window shutters open opposite her position and affording enough light to show her expression of disapproval.

'Watch your tongue.'

'Pa says it,' she said, her cheeks flushed with embarrassment and the shock of unexpectedly coming upon her mother.

'Pa should know better, as should you.'

Clara frowned and moved to the table, pulling out the nearside seat and sitting. 'The stitching has ripped open,' she stated after a few moments, holding the doll out towards her mother.

Lizbet narrowed her eyes and leant closer. She nodded and then turned to the view out of the window.

Clara took Rosie to her lap and idly toyed with the gap in the rear of the doll's dress.

'Leave it be. You'll only be making it worse,' said her mother, looking to the track that ran alongside South Field.

There was a brief silence. Clara studied her mother's shadowy profile, seeing a familiar light in her eye, like a distant star upon which wishes were made on cold and lonely nights.

'Bad dreams again?' asked the girl.

Lizbet gave a nod of response. 'You?' she asked, turning to her daughter.

'Uh-hu,' responded Clara.

'We make a fine pair.' A faint smile was raised upon her lips. She held her daughter's gaze momentarily and turned back to the view. The smile fell away and a pregnant silence followed, Clara noting the touch of grey in her mother's hair that had not been apparent prior to the departure of her father. Since that time the creases across her forehead and about her brown eyes had also deepened, his absence and her pining for his return making themselves known in her appearance.

'Pa'll be back,' said Clara, glancing out at the track diminishing in the shadows of the trees beyond the corn field, the crop ghostly in the dawn light. 'You mark my words.'

'They be marked and I pray they also be true.'

Clara slipped from her seat and stepped to her mother's side. 'Pa'll be back,' she repeated, placing her arms about her shoulders, Rosie still in hand.

Lizbet drew her daughter close, arm passing about her waist and leaning her head against the girl's hair. They shared a wordless embrace, crows cawing in the trees about the barn.

'Look!' whispered Lizbet.

Clara lifted her head and followed her mother's gaze out of the window. Standing upon the track was a solitary white-tailed deer, its small form like an apparition in the half-light. It was looking directly at them, ears rotated forward.

There were a few moments of stillness. The deer turned and moved to the boundary fence. It leapt in sudden motion, passing into the undergrowth beyond and out of sight.

Clara withdrew and her mother's arm fell away. 'I'm in need of the privy,' she stated. 'May I visit with Elsa when done?'

Lizbet looked to her daughter and saw the plea in her eyes. She sighed and nodded. 'If you must, but don't be going to the barn so dressed or you'll soil what was only washed yesterday.' She looked at the nightgown.

Clara's expression lifted and she bent forward to kiss her mother on the cheek. Turning, she went back to her room and changed into the dress she'd worn the previous day, tucking Rosie into the cord once it was tied about her waist.

Moving back into the hallway, she passed through the main room, flashing a smile at her mother as she made her way to the front door.

'Be sure you don't linger too long. I'll be in need of your assistance come sun up.'

'I won't,' she replied, opening the front door and passing out with eagerness.

Clara made her way around to the east side of the cottage and followed the path to the outhouse. 'Morning, Molly,' she said with a nod to the goat, who bleated in response as she sat amidst the grass beside the barn.

The trees rose ahead of her as she moved beyond the main buildings and reached the outhouse. She put her fingers through the hole in the door which acted as a handle. Shaking it on its hinges a moment, she looked for any sign of a rat and hoped that the noise had scared any that may have been in residence. She had long since learnt that they frequented the small building and wished no repeat of the fright she'd experienced when the lesson was taught.

Satisfied that any of the creatures would have made themselves scarce, she stepped inside and drew up the hem of her dress before seating herself over the hole in the wood. Relieving herself, she made a hasty exit from the deep gloom.

Clara passed onto the grass beside the path, veering towards the barn. She walked around to the front and slipped through the near door, hearing movement within the hutches as her entry gave a few of the rabbits a nervous start.

Ignoring the newly emptied cages, she walked towards the furthest on the shelf, gaze to the wire at the front but seeing no sign of Elsa in the deep shadows. Her pace became hurried as she worried her mother may have taken the rabbit, her heartbeat rising to match her steps.

Stopping before the hutch, she put her hands to the wire, fingers through its mesh as she leant forward and peered inside. She spied Elsa sitting upon the straw in the rear corner, largely hidden from sight by the darkness created by the wooden slats that made up the left third of the cage.

Taking a breath and grateful to have found her favoured rabbit alive and well, Clara turned the fastening and opened the door. Reaching inside, she picked Elsa up and carefully took her from the confinement.

'I was worried,' she stated, cuddling the rabbit close and rubbing her chin against the soft fur of its head.

Clara knelt upon the ground and settled Elsa onto her lap. She stroked its fur, finding pleasure in both the touch and motion.

'We done saw a deer upon the track,' she commented. 'I recall seeing a herd of them when Pa and me were seeking out firewood. They passed through the trees like spirits of the woods, making no sound and their fur golden in beams of sunlight. It were a fine sight.' She smiled down at the rabbit.

'It may be that seeing the deer was a sign that Pa be coming home,' she said, as much to herself as to Elsa. 'It come by to let us know.'

A brief disturbance in the hayloft caused her to look up over her shoulder. She could see nothing of concern in the meagre daylight, but kept her gaze to the deep shadows for a few moments.

'Probably a rat,' she commented, her smile fading as she turned back to the rabbit.

There was a gentle lowing and Clara looked over to the stall in the rear right corner. 'Seems Bella agrees,' she said, her expression brightening once again as she watched the cow tug hay from its feed bag, curved horns to either side of its forelock.

Stroking Elsa for a little longer, Clara then rose to her feet. Holding the rabbit around the midriff, she placed her back in the cage, the animal kicking with its back legs and knocking Rosie loose from the cord about her waist.

'I'll return later to feed you and clean out your cage,' she stated, closing the hutch and fastening the door before turning to the exit.

She walked over and passed out into the waking day. The dust of her passage thickened the air of the barn's interior, turning lackadaisically as it began to settle about the red-haired doll lying forlornly before the hutches.

7

Joshua stirred, the girl's voice coming to him as if from some half-remembered dream as it whispered through the eaves. He shifted, wincing with pain as he tried to discern what she was saying, but silence drew in.

Lying upon the straw, he listened intently and heard the vague padding of soft steps followed by the creak of hinges. Moving onto his side, he tried to push himself up, his arms threatening to give way as he struggled to sit.

With as little noise as possible, he moved closer to the edge of the hayloft, peering over to the floor below. There was no sign of occupation.

Wiping his brow, he pulled himself up using one of the roof supports. His arm around it, he tried to blink away dizziness, mind befuddled and thoughts clouded. His stomach moaned with hunger and he tried to focus his sight on the contents of the barn below. He knew he needed food, not only for sustenance, but in order to help his recovery.

His gaze settled on the hutches, their contents in shadow but the sound of scrabbling indicating that there were at least a few rabbits in residence. Licking his dry lips, he stepped away from the support, reluctantly releasing his hold as he moved to the steps.

Stumbling, Joshua fell to his knees, the sound making his shoulders tighten. Taking steadying breaths, he made his way on his hands and knees, body complaining with every movement.

Turning when he reached the top of the ladder, he took every care in descending. His legs trembled and sweat dampened his vest. He paused from time to time, resting against the rungs and closing his eyes, his mind swimming with pain, the solitary thought of needing food driving him on.

He reached the bottom and sagged against the ladder, gripping its sides tightly as his body was overcome with shaking. The effort was draining in his weakened state and he wondered if he would be able to make the climb back, glancing up to his place of refuge.

Joshua wiped his forehead and took a breath before shambling to the nearest hutch. He felt something soft beneath his foot and looked down as he moved it back. His brow furrowed as he stared down at the doll a moment, blinking to clear perspiration from his vision and thinking his mind may be playing tricks.

Bending and grimacing as pain shot through his back, he retrieved it from the dusty floor. He turned it in his hands, noting the stitches that had been pulled at the back of its blue dress.

His bleary gaze moved to the door, realising that the girl must have dropped it. He looked to the gaps in the slats that faced the cottage, seeking any sign that she was returning to collect her misplaced toy. He listened and watched for a while, wary and filled with tension.

Sounds of movement drew his gaze to the hutch and he spied the large rabbit within, its nose twitching as it caught his scent. Licking his lips as his mouth salivated, he reached for the cage door with his free hand.

His tremulous fingers stopped just shy of the latch, something inside causing the action to be truncated. He cocked his head to the side as he sought out the reason for the response, discovering a feeling deep within that warned him not to proceed.

Joshua glanced down at the doll and then looked along the row of hutches. He considered going to another, but the warning still arose from within.

Looking over his shoulder, he saw sacks against the wall on the opposite side of the barn. He turned and shuffled over, the cow in the stall lowing as the first rays of sunlight slid through the cracks in the slats above the hutches.

With the doll still in hand, he looked into one of the sacks nearest the cow's enclosure, seeing that he would be able to conceal himself between them and the stall should need arise. There were earthy potatoes inside and he took one up, greedily biting into it and chewing on the mouthful of vegetable and dried mud.

He pushed the rest into his mouth and undid the tie securing the next. Opening the neck of the sack, he found beets within and took out a couple, biting into one as soon as he were able.

Glancing to the front of the barn and seeing no sign of anyone passing before the slats, Joshua settled onto his knees as he chewed, cheeks bulging as he consumed the second beet and reached in for another. He settled back on his haunches and noted a loose thread hanging from the sack's opening. He reached for it as he continued to eat, pulling in order to extend its length before snapping it off. Lifting himself a little, he scanned the wall above the sacks and spied what he was looking for.

Stretching, he twisted the sliver of wood from the timber to which the slats were fastened. Resting back again, he used his dirty fingernails to create indents on either side of the splinter close to its thickest end.

He briefly set the thread and splinter upon his lap and reached for another potato. Taking a large bite, he put the remainder on the floor and lifted the doll to eye level. He turned it, hands still shaking but his activity distracting him from his poor condition. His mind addled and without thought of possible consequences, Joshua looked to the pulled stitches as the cow lowed once again and the regular chop of an axe arose from the direction of the cottage.

8

Clara put the next log on the block as her mother took a breath and readied the axe. Moving out of harms way, she watched the blade arc down, the sunlight flashing on its sharpness. The log split beneath its violence, the pieces tumbling to either side.

She took up another from the pile that her mother had cut the previous day and put it in place. The axe swung again and the head became embedded in the wood.

Lizbet put her foot to the log and levered the blade out with grunt of effort, pushing the handle away from her until the head came free with the squeak of metal against timber. She hefted the axe, her face showing the strain of the labour.

Bringing it to bare, the log split and she watched the pieces fall before tugging the blade from the block. 'It won't be long till harvest,' she commented, trying to take her mind from the growing ache in her arms and shoulders as her daughter put another log before her.

Clara glanced over her shoulder at South Field. 'It looks to be ready now.'

The axe arced. 'A few more days,' she said with an outward breath as the blade struck down.

'It may be Pa'll be back by then.' Clara knocked away one of the pieces which had spun and settled on the block, putting the next log in place.

'It may be so,' responded Lizbet, lifting the axe, 'but you shouldn't give yourself to hope.' The swing of the tool was punctuated by the crack of the log being forced apart.

Clara looked to her mother with an expression of consternation. 'You think he won't be back?'

Lizbet lowered the axe, resting its head on the ground and temporarily leaning on the handle. 'That not be what I said,' she replied, taking a rag that was tucked into the arm of her blouse and wiping her glistening face.

'Then what be your meaning?'

She saw the dismay of her daughter's expression and softened as she put the rag back in place. 'Only that you shouldn't be thinking he'll return when we see fit. He'll be home in due time.'

Lizbet gripped the handle and raised the axe in readiness, nodding to the block when Clara made no move to place another log upon it. Her daughter rested one before her and reached to her side as the axe arced downward, seeking comfort in Rosie's presence.

The discovery of the doll's absence coincided with the bite of the blade. She looked down in horror, the vacancy beneath the cord greeting her gaze.

'She be gone!' she blurted, turning her alarmed gaze to her mother.

Lizbet looked at her in confusion.

'Rosie's done fallen from the cord.'

'Where did you last be seeing her?' asked her mother.

'I don't know,' she said with a shake of her head. 'I be thinking she were tucked safe and sound.' She scanned the ground about her, the grass patchy and worn.

'I must have dropped her,' she stated, looking to the barn.

'Go look,' instructed Lizbet. 'You ain't been but two places since rising.'

She straightened and then looked to her mother. 'What about the wood cutting?'

'I can manage,' replied Lizbet. 'The mule's load has already been done.'

Clara hesitated and then turned, following the path in front of the house and then taking the branch which took her between cottage and barn. She passed Molly on her way to the outhouse, all the time scanning the ground in the hope of spying Rosie, the goat looking on with blades of grass poking from the sides of her mouth.

Walking over to the small building, she opened the door and peered inside, rattling it as she did so. Seeing no sign of the doll and with nose wrinkling, she stepped to the commode and tentatively leant out over the hole in order to try and see into the darkness below.

There was no evidence of Rosie and Clara gratefully exited into the sunlight. She passed back between the buildings and went to the barn doors, pausing to glance at the grass to either side.

Pulling open the left-hand door, she stepped in and looked to the floor in front of the hutches. Seeing nothing, she scanned the interior, her gaze attracted by a touch of red on the opposite side of the barn. She spied Rosie lying by the sacks leaning against the wall and her expression became one of puzzlement.

'How'd you be getting yourself over there?' she asked as she walked over and picked up the doll, sure that she hadn't strayed so far from the hutches. 'I thought I'd done lost you,' she added as she looked at the bright smile upon Rosie's face.

Her brow creased as her fingers came into contact with something unfamiliar. Turning the doll around, Clara discovered that the tear in the seam had been repaired with rough cord. She stared at the mend in confusion, shaking her head and looking about the interior in the hope of solving the mystery.

Briefly glancing at Bella, she slowly turned back to the doors. She pondered the events of the morning, sure that her mother had not stitched up the gap before she'd left the house.

With another shake of her head, she exited the building and wandered over to where her mother was chopping the last of the wood. The axe bit down as she came to a stop by the porch.

'I'm glad to see Rosie be safe and well,' said Lizbet with a smile and a glance, returning her gaze to her daughter when Clara's expression registered in her mind. 'What be the matter?'

Clara stared at the doll and then lifted her gaze. 'Did you be mending the tear?' she asked with uncertainty.

'What tear?' asked Lizbet, leaning forward and removing the pieces from the block before putting another log in place.

Clara held the doll out to her mother so she could see the back of its dress. 'She were lying on the floor in the barn, but the tear has been mended.'

Lizbet looked at the repair and then readied the axe. 'So it has.'

'But you didn't mend it.'

The log split in two and the pieces fell to the sides. 'You must have done so,' she responded, pausing in her task. 'Seems as though it not just be a long count of years that affects the memory, but a short count too,' she said with a smile.

'I didn't,' said Clara with a shake of her head.

'She ain't done mended herself now, has she? She wouldn't have been able to reach, for a start,' she joked. 'You must've made the mend when you changed into your dress.'

She stared at the doll in befuddlement, her mouth slightly open and expression filled with confusion. 'I sure as day don't remember doing it,' she responded, her mother's attempt at humour passing unnoticed.

'If that be the case, it must have been the faerie folk.' Lizbet raised the axe and set about the chopping once again.

Clara remained silent for a while, thoughtfully running her thumb over the rough cord. 'You think it could be so?' she asked eventually.

'I ain't done mended it, so if you didn't they must have seen to it.'

'You think faerie folk be real?'

Lizbet shrugged. 'There be a great many things of strangeness and mystery in this world,' she said as she swung the axe to split the last of the logs, 'and I ain't seen nothing to say they don't exist.'

Clara pondered as her mother left the axe resting in the block and wiped her face with the rag from her sleeve. Lizbet saw her daughter's continuing bemusement and stepped over, holding out her hand.

'Let me be taking a closer look,' she said.

Clara passed her the doll and Lizbet studied the stitching thoughtfully.

'There be some skill in the mend, even though it be done with sackcloth,' she said with an approving nod. 'There be faerie folk abiding in the barn for sure.'

'Truly?' Clara looked at her dubiously as her mother handed Rosie back to her.

Lizbet nodded again. 'There ain't no doubt. The dress couldn't have done stitched itself now, could it?'

Clara was still unconvinced, but no other answer to the riddle of how the dress had been mended presented itself.

'Come, help me carry these in,' said Lizbet, bending and beginning to gather the timber into her arms, certain that her daughter had simply forgotten making the mend. Tiredness often addled the mind and both of them had been disturbed by bad dreams which had caused them to rise early.

Still far from satisfied, Clara tucked Rosie into the cord at her waist and moved to help her mother. She began to pick up the wood, placing it in the crook of her left arm as her thoughts lingered on the mystifying discovery. She glanced over her shoulder at the barn, deciding further investigation was needed, though it would have to wait until she'd finished her chores.

9

She stood on the porch and watched as her mother walked away along the track beside South Field. She had been asked if she wanted to visit with old Harold Tyler, but had declined the offer of accompanying her mother in the delivery of the rabbit furs.

Clara raised her hand in farewell when Lizbet glanced back over her shoulder. Waiting until she passed out of sight beyond the strand of trees, she turned to look at the barn. Her stomach churned lightly with nerves as her thoughts became focussed on the mystery of Rosie's mended dress once again.

She began towards the building, the fall of her feet gentle upon the dry earth and flattened grass. Her tension rose and she was soon creeping along the path, barely daring to blink as she looked to the slats of the walls and then concentrated on the doors ahead of her.

Reaching them, Clara paused with her hand to the handle. She pulled and the creak of hinges announced her arrival, the noise causing her to wince.

She leant forward and peered in. The sun was high in the western sky and its beams lanced the gloom. Bella stirred in the rear right stall, looking over and flapping her ears at the irritation of a fly as soft sounds arose from some of the hutches.

Clara stepped inside, leaving the door open behind her. She looked to the few sacks leant against the wall opposite the hutches, staring at the shadowy gaps between and seeking sign of unusual activity.

Glancing around, she could see no other obvious place where faerie folk would hide and so walked over to the vegetables, passing through shafts of sunlight and dust swirling in her wake. Moving to the near side, she crouched and stared into the darkness between the sacks and wall, seeing nothing of note.

'Are you there?' she whispered.

No response was forthcoming and she straightened. Frowning, her gaze settled on the hutches across from her. 'I'd best see to your bedding,' she commented, thinking of no other course of action she could take in order to detect the presence of faeries.

Clara fetched the hand barrow from between the stalls and placed it before the rabbits. Going to Elsa's cage, she opened the door and lifted the creature out. 'Time for you to be having new straw,' she said, stroking its head and transferring it to the empty hutch on the floor beneath, its water trough following after.

Straining as she took up Elsa's cage, she turned and tipped it over the barrow. Straw and faeces fell from the open door. She shook it to empty the last and then replaced it upon the shelf.

She moved along the hutches and repeated the process, the remaining rabbits placed in empty hutches so theirs could be cleared of the soiled bedding. Reaching the end of the row and finishing the task, she took the barrow to the doors and passed out of the barn.

Clara took it to the rear of the building and added the contents to a pile of waste that rested before the trees. Returning to the interior, she took the barrow back between the stalls and left it facing the wall, Bella watching as she chewed on some hay.

Taking to the ladder, Clara climbed to the loft. She went to the much diminished pile of straw, keeping her head low despite her stature, there being enough clearance for her to walk without fear of banging her head. She gathered up an armful from the edge and carried it back to the barn floor, placing it inside Elsa's hutch.

She fetched the rabbit out of her temporary home and stood for a while with the docile creature in her arms. 'You're so soft,' she stated as she stroked her and looked to the dainty nose that twitched on occasion, 'and cute as a button,' she added with a passing smile.

Elsa announced her wish to be released with a strong kick of her rear legs and was placed back in her cage. Clara turned the fastening and peered in through the wire before passing over to the sacks and taking out one of the beets.

'Here,' she stated, briefly opening the door to place the food inside.

Elsa hopped over and sniffed at the offering before beginning to eat.

Clara made her way back up the ladder and into the hayloft. She recalled how it had been fit to burst after the previous year's harvest and they'd had to store the excess where the barrow now rested beneath her. Despite the irritation to her skin, she had helped her father carry it in with enthusiasm, enjoying his company, which was always filled with fooling and mischief. They had laughed until they'd cried at her scarecrow appearance when the day was done, strands of straw in her hair and caught upon her dress.

She crouched and began to take up handfuls from the boards, a smile upon her face as she reminisced.

Her heart leapt in response to sudden movement in the straw before her hand. She stared with wide eyes, discerning a darkened food amidst the stalks.

Slowly turning to her left, she peered into the shadows below the eaves of the corner. Her chest was filled with thunder as she spied a figure resting in the straw.

Clara moved back in alarm, body trembling.

'Wait!' whispered the man as he reached out to her, his torso rising from its partial concealment, face moving into a beam of sunlight but the shadows remaining as if clinging to his countenance.

Clara stumbled and fell onto her rump. She began to scrabble backwards on the straw-strewn boards, eyes wide as she regarded him with fear.

'I done mended your doll,' he stated, pointing at Rosie.

She slowed her retreat and came to a stop a short distance from the ladder. 'It were you?'

Joshua nodded. 'I done found her at first light.'

She cocked her head to the side as she regarded him, noting the broad nose and full lips, his eyebrows thick and dark stubble rising to his cheekbones.

'You've no cause to fear me, Miss.'

Clara got to her feet, keeping a wary eye on him at all times. She backed to the top of the steps and took hold of the sides, carefully putting her right foot to the top rung.

'Please,' he pleaded, his eyes begging her to remain. 'I done hear the song you be singing on your visit to the crick the morning previous. It were a sweet tune and pleasing to the ears.' Joshua forced a smile, sitting up straight and wincing with the pain. He felt nauseous and dizzy, but fought through it in order to converse with the girl.

'You heard me?' she asked, halting her descent.

Joshua nodded. 'I be a hiding in the reeds,' he replied. 'Be Rosie the doll's name?'

Clara gave a nod. 'Be you one of the faerie folk?'

He looked at her curiously and then shook his head. 'Just a man,' he replied.

She rose from the ladder and moved a little closer. 'I ain't never done seen the likes of you before,' she stated.

'You ain't never been away from this here farm?' he asked in surprise.

'I ain't never been more than a couple of miles, to Tyler's farm,' she replied. 'Harold is an old crank, crooked and in need of a stick by which to walk. He chews tobaccy and the stains of his spitting cover his yard in dry times, like some sickness of the ground.'

'You truly never seen others like me?'

She shook her head as she crouched. 'You say you're just a man?'

'Just a man,' he confirmed.

Clara sidled forward, remaining wary. Reaching towards his foot, she regularly glanced towards him, alert to any sign of danger. Her fingers tentatively touched his ankle. She rubbed the skin briefly with the tip of her thumb, looking to see if the colour had been removed, believing that he may be dirty or stained somehow.

'Flesh and blood, just like you, Miss,' he said.

She withdrew her hand and turned to study his face. 'How long you been up here?' she asked, noting the hollows beneath his cheekbones and the glisten of perspiration.

'Since the day just passed,' he replied, swallowing against his sickness and blinking as his vision swam momentarily.

'Why ain't you home? Have you a wife and children?'

'I…' Joshua struggled to think of a suitable answer, his mind sluggish under the influence of his condition.

'You been in the war?' she asked before he could respond further, noting the dark stain of blood at the side of his vest, leaning forward slightly to try and see his back. 'It may be you fought alongside my Pa.'

Joshua looked at her in surprise. 'Your Pa be fighting for the Union?'

Clara's expression became one of disgust as she shook her head. 'For the Confederacy,' she stated with pride.

'I ain't been in no war,' he said.

'You sure looks like you have.'

'Be it only you and your Ma living here?' he enquired.

She nodded. 'Ma and Pa be moving out here eleven year ago from Jefferson City,' she replied. 'I were born in the house. Old Mrs Tyler came to help with the birth, but I don't be recalling her. She passed before I done took my first step.'

'Pa'll be back when the war be won,' she added. 'Maybe you can help with the harvest while he be away, like you done helped with Rosie?' She looked at him expectantly.

'Where be your Ma now?' he asked, glancing past her.

'She be visiting with Old Harold. If I knows the way he likes to talk, she'll be gone a good while yet.'

Joshua shifted in attempt to ease his discomfort. 'I don't be supposing you've any food?'

'There be a little stew from supper,' replied Clara. 'Rabbit stew,' she clarified, her expression falling.

'It'd be a kindness if I could be having me some, Miss.'

'Clara,' she stated.

'Miss Clara,' he said with a nod. 'My name be Joshua Andrew.' He held out his hand.

She looked at it, his fingers trembling. Tentatively taking hold, they shook hands in greeting and Joshua sagged after their connection was undone.

'I'll be fetching the stew,' she said, seeing his weakened state and standing, head bowed as if the weight of the roof pressed down upon her.

Joshua nodded. 'Much obliged, Miss Clara.' He forced a thin smile.

She continued to look down upon him a moment and then made her way to the ladder. Turning to make her descent, she stared into the corner, his ragged appearance and the darkness of his skin filling her with curiosity which she hoped to satiate upon her return.

10

Clara stepped out of the cottage carrying a bowl containing the last of the stew. Her gaze went to where the track passed south through the trees, but there was no sign of her mother returning.

She walked along the path back to the barn, feeling excited by the prospect of seeing Joshua again. His presence was a curiosity and she hoped to discover his origins. She had no clue as to why he had chosen to abide there nor as to how long he intended to stay.

Entering, she made her way over to the ladder and climbed up, her progress hampered by the bowl in her hand. Reaching the top, she went over to him as he sat hunched beneath the eaves.

'Here,' she stated, crouching and holding out the bowl, a piece of bread leaning against the side as it rested on the stew.

Joshua straightened, his expression tightening and teeth gritted against the aches and pains. He reached forward and took the bowl with a nod of gratitude.

'How long will you be resting here?' asked Clara as he tore off a piece of bread and dipped it into the meagre leftovers at the bottom of the bowl.

He shook his head as he pushed the dripping bread into his mouth. 'I know not,' he answered through the food. 'My strength must be recovered before anything else be done.'

'I could speak with Ma. She may allow you to remain if you help harvest the corn.'

He looked up at her sharply, his eyes raw and surrounded by shadows which spoke of his ill health. 'It best you don't be speaking of me to your Ma, Miss Clara.'

She stared at him with brow creased. 'Why? What harm could come of it?'

Joshua swallowed as he thought. 'She may not take kindly to my presence,' he replied, '"specially seeing as I'm here without permit.'

Clara pondered, looking down at the floor before her as she scratched her arm. 'I could be telling her I done said you could stay.'

'It be best not to be saying a word,' he said. 'It can be our secret,' he added conspirationally, breaking off another piece and mopping up more of the stew, his hunger demanding to be satiated.

Clara nodded as he stuffed the food into his mouth, not convinced of the wisdom of secrecy and made unhappy by the thought of deceiving her mother. 'Where be your home?' she asked, wishing to change the direction of their conversation.

Joshua chewed a moment, looking down at the meagre contents of the bowl. 'I've no place to be calling home.'

'Then surely it be better if I talk to Ma. I see no reason for her to take against you being here and reckon she'd be happy with the help when reaping comes.'

Joshua shook his head vigorously. 'You mustn't say a word, Miss Clara,' he stated, holding her gaze. 'Promise me.'

She hesitated and then nodded. Joshua continued to stare at her awhile before devouring the rest of the food. She watched him, wondering at his background. Her gaze moved to the stain of blood at the side of his vest and she considered the possibility that he was a deserter from the army.

'How be the stew?' she asked, deciding to keep his presence to herself for the time being and hoping to discern more of his origins.

'Mmm,' he responded with a nod, licking his lips and running the final piece of bread around the inside of the bowl to collect up the last of the meal. 'Your Ma cooks well.'

'It be good country cooking,' said Clara as he put the bowl on the boards in front of him. 'Pa say it were why he married her,' she added jokingly.

'It be a good reason, true enough,' he responded with a smile.

'Clara!'

Joshua stiffened and Clara looked over her shoulder at the sound of her mother's call.

'I must be on my way,' she said, getting to her feet. 'I'd best leave the bowl. If she see me carrying it, there are sure to be enquiries.'

'And you ain't going to tell her I be lodging here?'

Clara shook her head. 'I'll try and visit later. I've yet to clear Bella's stall and so must return.'

Joshua gave a nod. 'Can you be bringing more food?'

She looked down at the floor, not comfortable with sneaking around behind her mother's back. 'I'll try,' she conceded. 'If I were to tell...'

'You can't, Miss Clara,' he interrupted, a desperate plea in his dark eyes.

She frowned. 'I'll hold my tongue,' she conceded.

'Clara?'

She turned and went to the ladder, her mother's voice nearer the barn as she tried to discern her daughter's whereabouts. 'In the barn,' she called back with a final look to the unusual man before passing down the rungs.

The doors opened as she reached the bottom and she looked to her mother. 'I be just cleaning the hutches.'

Lizbet looked to the cages and saw that some had their doors open, the soiled bedding in clear sight. 'It seems the chore goes slowly.'

'There was a rat,' she said with a glance back at the hayloft.

'It ain't the first time you've seen one of those and it sure won't be the last.'

'After what done happened in the privy...' responded Clara, leaving the sentence unfinished and lowering her gaze.

Lizbet regarded her daughter's downcast expression a moment and softened. 'Are you in want of my help?'

She shook her head. 'It be gone now,' she replied. 'How fares Mr Tyler?'

'Same as always. His bunions be acting up again and he reckons rain must be a coming.'

Clara gave a nod of response. 'I'll be finishing with the cages and then clean the stall, unless there be something you have need of me for.'

'I'll go check on the east fields and return to prepare supper,' said Lizbet with a shake of her head. 'Will you be wanting to finish the stew from last night? I could warm it through.'

She blushed. 'I already done eaten it,' she stated. 'I were hankering for something and didn't think you'd pay any mind to me having the remainder.'

'You didn't think to wait until I be returning?' Lizbet regarded her with disapproval.

Clara hung her head in response, but offered no further words of explanation.

'Will you still be wanting supper?'

She gave a nod, feeling guilty at the deception and unable to lift her gaze to meet her mother's.

Lizbet regarded her a moment longer and then turned to exit the barn. 'I'll be back shortly,' she said as she stepped out, leaving the doors ajar.

Clara listened to her mother's receding steps. Feeling the weight of the lie upon her shoulders, she turned to the ladder and stared up at the hayloft. With a frown, she took hold of the sides and began up to collect more straw for the rabbits.

'Don't speak loudly,' she whispered when she rose above the edge and Joshua's vague presence drew into sight.

'My thanks for not telling your mother, Miss Clara.'

Her frown deepened. She moved to the straw and began to gather it into her arms. Joshua watched, seeing the unhappy expression upon her face.

'I wouldn't ask you to lie unless the need was great,' he stated earnestly.

Clara didn't respond, the confirmation of what she'd done adding to the weight that kept her head low. She moved back to the ladder and descended without giving him another glance. Reaching the floor, she went straight to the hutches and placed clean bedding into those with their doors open before putting the rabbits back inside.

Going between the stalls, she looked in on Bella, checking to see if the injury to her shin had fully healed. It seemed in good repair and Clara decided to turn the beast out even though the day was waning, her enforced confinement having lasted over a week.

Taking a length of rope hanging from a bent nail in the support beside her, she opened the gate and stepped over to the cow, Bella licking the end of her glistening nose and swishing her tail. Clara distractedly scratched her forelock and then tied the rope about her broad neck. She began to lead her out, gaze turning to the doors and glad to be making her exit from the barn, finding the enclosure increasingly claustrophobic.

Pushing the doors wide, she led Bella out into the sunlight. She made her way towards the strand of trees to the right, intending to tether the cow in the grasses between them and the east fields that they masked from sight. She didn't glance back, but her thoughts turned to Joshua's presence and she wondered whether she should tell her mother despite his protests.

Reaching no conclusion, she passed beneath the boughs and listened to the brush of leaves in the breeze. The trees seemed to be whispering the answer, but she could not grasp their meaning as she moved through the shadows and Bella sedately followed.

11

They ate in silence, Clara having taken the seat opposite the window, the shutters open on the evening. The colours of sunset rested upon ripples of thin cloud stretching to the south as roosting birds called into the stillness. The sounds and vivid display of day's demise were in stark contrast to the gloomy hush gathered within the cottage as mother and daughter consumed the meal of mutton and boiled vegetables.

Lizbet watched as Clara toyed with her beans, elbow on the table and head resting on her hand. 'Be something bothering you?' she asked, her daughter's fork becoming still.

'I'm tired,' responded Clara unconvincingly.

'Well, them beans ain't gonna leap into your mouth all by themselves.'

She looked down at the vegetables without enthusiasm. 'I ain't very hungry.'

'That'll be the stew you done finished earlier.' Lizbet's tone contained a reprimand.

Clara didn't respond and kept her gaze to the plate. Her appetite had been stolen by the situation in which she found herself. She was at a loss as to what she should do. Joshua had requested her silence in earnest and she believed there was more to his plea than he had revealed. At the same time, she did not want to continue deceiving her mother, an act which brought with it the heaviness of guilt and regret.

'Finish the meat and you may be excused,' said Lizbet, interrupting the girl's thoughts.

Clara glanced up and gave a nod. She cut the remaining piece of mutton in half and stabbed the left portion with her fork. Placing it into her mouth, she chewed on the meat, finding no pleasure in its consumption.

Lizbet watched, her daughter's demeanour noticeably dejected, shoulders drawn inward and head bowed. 'I know it be a little tough,' she commented. 'Tyler had slaughtered his eldest yew and the years show in the meat.'

'Geraldine,' she said, swallowing the food.

'Pardon?' Lizbet looked at her in confusion.

'His eldest ewe, she were called Geraldine.' Clara stabbed the last piece.

'What've I said about naming…?'

'I didn't name her, he did,' she interrupted with a glance, 'and he be farming much longer than you,' she added pointedly before placing the mutton in her mouth.

Lizbet's expression tightened. She looked at her daughter, but made no further comment. Something was clearly gnawing at Clara and her challenging words were like bait. If she bit, there was sure to be an argument.

'Be there anything you need to do when supper's done?' she asked, taking the politic route of changing the subject.

Clara stared at the beans remaining on her plate. 'Feed the rabbits,' she stated after a pause.

Lizbet glanced out of the window. 'If you be done with the beans, you'd better pass to the barn before it gets dark.'

Clara hesitated and it seemed for a moment that she was about to put voice to what troubled her, taking a breath in readiness. Her shoulders sagging upon the exhale, she put her fork down on the plate, deciding to hold her silence.

Pushing back her chair, she rose and went to the stove. 'Can I take the rest for the rabbits?' she asked, peering at the remaining beans in the cooking pot and then looking to her mother.

'Ain't there alfalfa left?'

'I thought they may be hankering for a change,' she lied.

Lizbet studied her daughter and then nodded.

Clara scraped the last of her beans into the pot and then placed her plate on the cabinet to the right. Taking up the cooking pot, she made her way around the table to the front door, opening it and passing out without another word, her mother staring after her and listening to her receding steps in thoughtfulness.

She approached the barn and her mood continued to darken. Going inside, her gaze immediately rose to the hayloft, her jaw clenched as she made her way to the ladder with barely a glance at the rabbit hutches lining the wall.

With awkwardness brought about by the cooking pot's carriage, she made the ascent with slow steps. The ladder creaked as her head lifted over the edge and she looked to the shadows in the corner. Joshua's vague form could be seen lying amidst the straw, his lower half all but hidden beneath.

Stepping onto the boards, she made her way over with head bowed. 'I've brung you some beans,' she announced.

There was no response and no evidence of movement.

Clara halted before him and crouched, narrowing her eyes as she stared at his face, the growing gloom making his features hard to determine. Discerning that his eyes were closed, she set the pot down and reached for his near shoulder. 'Joshua?' she said, touching the stained vest.

He mumbled and shifted, face becoming pinched. 'I didn't do it,' he stated, his words sluggish and ill-defined.

She looked upon him a moment and then touched his shoulder again, giving a gentle push. 'Joshua?'

His lids slowly lifted. He found his vision blurred and blinked to try and gain clarity. He attempted to lift his head, but dizziness overcame him and he let it sink back to the straw. Pain caused him to grit his teeth, his back filled with greater agonies than before and his state seemingly becoming worse rather than improving.

'I've beans for you.'

'Beans?' He forced his mind to fight through the mental distortion and tried to focus.

Clara reached down and tipped the pot towards him so that he could see the contents. 'I couldn't be getting anything else,' she explained.

Joshua nodded vaguely, struggling to hold his centre, the periphery of his mind thrown into chaos by the waning of his condition and threatening to overcome the precarious grasp he held on the world about him. 'Water?' he asked, licking his lips.

'I'll fetch you some,' she stated, rising and turning for the ladder.

She made her way to the ladder, worry having replaced her previous pensiveness. He was clearly being subdued by the ills that plagued him, his face covered in perspiration and paled in comparison with their previous encounter. The light of his eyes had dimmed and he had a stupefied look which reminded her of her father after partaking of his special drink.

Clara backed onto the rungs and looked over at him as she descended. He passed beyond sight and she soon reached the floor. She went to the pail resting beside the lines of hutches, glancing into Elsa's, but unable to see the creature in the darkness of her enclosure.

Looking around for a suitable drinking vessel, she stepped to the nearest empty cage. She took out the small water trough, unhooking it from bent nails that held it in place. Dropping it into the pail, she lifted the bucket and went back to the steps, her arm straining and the wash of water causing it to sway with increasing strength.

She began up, trying to still the pail, the change of motion causing a spill down her leg. Frowning, she felt the coolness seeping into her dress and running down her shin, a brief chill causing her shoulders to tremble.

Clara went back to his side, her nostrils flaring as she neared and caught a foul scent in the still air. Joshua had soiled himself in her absence and her concern grew in light of his obvious weakness.

Crouching, she found that his eyes had closed. 'I done brung the water you asked for, Joshua.'

His eyes opened a little and he fought to find focus. Clara shuffled forward and gathered water in the tin trough. Placing her free hand beneath his head, she raised it and dribbled some into his mouth. Much of it spilt down the sides and upon his chin, the droplets darkening the straw.

She repeated the process a couple more times and then Joshua shook his head, closing his eyes once again. She lowered it and removed her hand before placing the trough back into the bucket. Staring down at him, the need to tell her mother grew stronger. He was clearly in want of nursing and she had not the skill to do so.

'I'm of a mind to be telling Ma that you abide here,' she said into the gathering dark. 'Your condition declines and she may be able to help.'

'No,' he croaked, forcing the word out, his lids remaining shut.

'But you worsen,' she protested.

He opened his eyes and stared at her, seeing only the blurred shadow of her presence. 'Please,' he managed, coughing briefly, his expression filled with tension and perspiration dripping down the sides of his face, his short black hair glistening with its dampness and woven with straw.

'Ma could treat you,' she stated, a plea in her tone. 'If I tell her we be friends and you done mended Rosie, then there ain't gonna be no issue with you abiding in the barn.'

With great effort, Joshua reached out and took hold of her forearm, his muscles filled with aching tightness. 'Please, Miss Clara,' he rasped.

She held his gaze, his dark eyes sickened and filled with pain, their light dulled. Nodding her agreement, she felt torn and at odds with what appeared to be the right course of action in the circumstances.

Joshua's hand fell away and he closed his eyes again, his breathing laboured. She watched for a while, certain that he had been overcome by his sickness and fallen into sleep.

Rising, Clara made her way to the ladder, leaving the pail beside him in case he woke and was in want of refreshment. She began the descent, looking for him in the darkness, but finding little hint as to his presence as night took hold.

12

Lizbet lay upon her cot and listened to the indistinct sound of her daughter's voice. She had taken to talking softly with Rosie on nights when she was particularly distressed, the first time being after her father had gone to war.

She recalled hearing the vagaries of her daughter conversing as she'd walked up the hall towards her room after shedding many a tear over Walter's departure. She'd passed to the other side of the hall and listened at Clara's door, hearing a one-sided discussion concerning the likelihood of her father facing danger and of his return. She'd entered and gone to Clara's cot, the two of them finding solace in a tearful embrace.

She stared at the ceiling and pondered what could be disturbing her daughter. There had been no scolding and there was nothing else she could think of that could have caused Clara to become unduly worried or upset.

Thinking over the day, she identified her return from Tyler's farm as the point of change. Clara's mood had clearly shifted since she'd left and she wondered what could have happened during her time away.

Rolling onto her side and staring into the darkness with a thoughtful expression, she tried to solve the puzzle, but found no scenario that fitted the events of the day. She had asked Clara if she wanted to accompany her and the girl had been genuinely disinclined. There had been no sign of hurt or injury and she had made no complaint of feeling unwell. No reason became apparent for the melancholia that had struck her daughter and now caused her to converse with the doll as a means of finding comfort.

The sounds of talking were replaced by the soft hum of the song she had made up for her doll. Lizbet sighed, the tune carrying with it a sense of loneliness. She briefly thought about her daughter's lack of interaction with other children and wished that their attempts at having another child had borne fruit. Had they been successful, Clara would have had a sibling with whom to spend time, but it was not to be.

Her mind turned to Walter and she wondered if he were thinking of her. She pictured him lying in a tent or seated behind a spiked redoubt, flanked by other Missouri guerrillas as he kept watch with his rifle in hand.

The rumble of distant thunder passed through the cottage and she imagined cannon fire and smoke, a battlefield littered with bodies. She tried to push the image from her mind, turning once again as another rumble reverberated through the heavens.

The door to her room creaked and she looked over, able to see the faint paleness of her daughter's nightgown.

'Can I sleep with you?' The gentle plea was filled with trepidation.

'Yes,' she answered, moving over and pulling back the cover.

Clara came to the bed with Rosie cuddled to her chest. She drew into her mother as Lizbet pulled the cover over her fragile form.

'The thunder?' asked Lizbet in a whisper, in truth glad for the company after the disturbing thoughts of war.

She felt her daughter nod as she put her arm about her shoulders. 'It will pass,' she stated, staring upward, the ceiling hidden from sight as the storm continued to announce its approach.

13

Clara stirred and opened her eyes upon the emptiness beside her. She reached out beneath the cover and felt the fading warmth indicating that her mother had not risen long before.

Yawning and stretching, she wiped a tear from her cheek and looked to the shutters. Daylight was visible between, though she could not tell if the sun had yet to rise or if the clouds that had rolled in during the night remained to blanket the day.

With Rosie held to her chest, she swung her legs over the side of the cot and felt the chill morning air against her skin. She stood and went to the door, stepping out into the hallway beyond. Turning towards the main room, she discovered her mother silhouetted in the entrance to the cottage and her expression became one of curiosity.

As she approached, her gaze moved to the field at the front of the house and she discovered the reason for her mother's presence in the doorway. The corn had been flattened by the downpour that had pelted upon the roof as the storm passed over, the thunder quaking to the bone and flashes of light piecing the night with violent illumination.

Clara went to her mother's side and they both stared out at the damage. 'Will it rise again if there be no more rain?' she asked without turning from the sight, a few patches still standing amidst the devastation.

'I know not,' responded Lizbet with a defeated tone. 'Harvesting was only days away,' she said with a shake of her head.

Clara glanced at the sky and found it clear of cloud, the sky above the trees to the east with a touch of gold as the sun neared the horizon. 'It may be just the weight of the water that hold the stalks down,' she suggested. 'The sun'll dry them and they'll be up in the flick of a fish's tail,' she added hopefully, looking at her mother's profile.

'They be beaten down by the rain,' responded Lizbet, shaking her head again and turning from the field. 'Beaten and broken.'

Clara watched her go to the table and seat herself with her back to the window, the shutters still closed. Wishing to brighten her mother's mood, Clara went to open them, reaching for the latch.

'No!' she said sharply, her daughter's hand falling still. 'That ain't a sight I want to be seeing again until I'm good and ready.'

Clara's arm fell to her side and she made her way to the table after a pause. She seated herself to the right of her mother, the chimneybreast at her back, and tried to think of something to say that would alleviate her concerns.

'Without the corn we'll have no bread and no grain for feed or barter,' said her mother before she could find the right words.

'We don't knows that we'll be without it yet,' she responded.

'What we salvage won't be enough.'

'What about the east fields?'

Lizbet turned to her. 'They won't have fared any better,' she said. 'That storm be the end of our hope for a good harvest.'

'I still hope,' offered Clara.

Lizbet reached out and took hold of her daughter's arm, giving it a gentle squeeze, but saying nothing further. Releasing her, she rose from her seat and went to the cabinet by the stove, lifting the lid of the wooden bread bin and taking out the remainder of the loaf within.

They proceeded to break the fast in silence, partaking of bread and goat's cheese. Clara ached to say something of comfort, but nothing suitable was forthcoming. She looked beyond her mother as she chewed, staring at the faint strands of sunlight lying across the battered corn as they seeped through the strand of trees to the east. She hoped to see improvement as the day lengthened, prayed that the warmth and light would begin to raise the stalks until they stood proud once more.

'The sun will bring the crop new vigour,' stated Clara, trying to sound upbeat. 'I reckon the harvest will still fare well.'

Lizbet chewed and swallowed her food in brooding deliberation before turning to her daughter. 'Mildew and rot will set in before we can harvest all,' she said sadly. 'If we had more hands maybe there be a chance, but Tyler has his own harvest to reap and there ain't no other for a long count of miles.'

Clara's thoughts turned to Joshua. If her mother could tend him and bring him back to health, then his aid could see them clear to bringing the harvest in. There was only one choice open to her now; to tell her mother. That act would not only help end his suffering, but would also give them a fighting chance of gathering the corn before too much was lost. She would visit with him and tell him of her decision before informing her mother of his presence, wanting the opportunity to explain and hoping that he would understand.

She rose from her seat with sudden urgency. 'I'll go check the rabbits,' she stated over her shoulder as she hastily made for the door.

'Not until you've changed,' responded Lizbet.

Clara glanced down at her nightgown in frustration. Any delay would be a delay in returning Joshua to fitness, something they could ill afford if her mother was right and the corn would not rise again.

She hastened to her room and stripped off the gown after throwing Rosie to the cot. Taking up the pale green dress hung over the foot of the bed, she let it fall over her head and was already making her way back along the hallway as she tied the cord about her waist.

'Don't be long. There's sweeping to be done,' said her mother as she padded across the main room.

'I won't,' she responded as she passed out of the doorway.

Clara followed the path to the barn, her steps quickening until she was running for the doors. She hurried inside and her gaze immediately went to the hayloft as she passed across the dusty floor and took hold of the ladder's sides. Her foot slipped on a rung in her haste to reach the top and she winced as her shin jarred against the wood.

Face flushed with pain, she reached the top and searched for him in the shadows, the last vestige of night seemingly gathered in the corner and concealing Joshua from sight. She moved to where the pail rested as her vision adjusted to the gloom.

'Joshua?' she said softly, able to make out his glistening countenance, eyes closed and face contorted by the malady that gripped him so tightly.

There was no response as she crouched beside him.

'Joshua!' she said with greater volume.

He groaned, but did not wake.

She reached forward and prodded his shoulder, feeling the dampness of his vest beneath her fingertip. 'I need to be speaking with you.'

Joshua's brow became taught, his body wrung out by his torment in sweats and contractions. A spasm caused his arms and legs to quiver and he let out a moan.

Clara stared at him. The worsening of his condition was plain to see and she feared he would not wake no matter how much encouragement she gave.

Rising, she turned and made for the ladder with a determined stride. The choice she'd made had become all the more steadfast in light of his failing health. She had to tell her mother or both Joshua and the crop could be lost.

14

Clara ran into the house and found her mother still seated at the table. She stepped over and stood before the nearside chair, catching her breath as she did so.

Lizbet looked to her daughter, her expression one of intrigue. 'How do the rabbits fare?' she asked, fearing the storm had caused further damage.

Clara took another breath and gathered herself in readiness to reveal what she must 'There be a man of shadows in the barn,' she blurted.

Lizbet looked at her in confusion. 'A man of shadows?'

She nodded. 'He may be one of the faerie folk,' she stated, gripping the back of the chair before her. 'He were hiding in the shadows of the hayloft and they clung to him when he moved into the light. He done mended Rosie and be needing your help,' she said, the words tumbling out breathlessly.

Lizbet continued to study her daughter and then looked out of the open door, her brow furrowed as she tried to unriddle what she'd be told. 'What sort of help?'

'He ain't well. Something diresome grips him.'

She turned back to Clara, unable to fathom what her daughter was talking about.

'He say his name be Joshua Andrew.' She stepped to her mother and took hold of her hand. 'You have to help him,' she said with a gentle tug.

'One of the faerie folk?' asked Lizbet, the question filled with doubt.

'Come and see for yourself.'

Lizbet let herself be guided from the chair, rising and making her way out onto the porch. Her daughter's insistence drew her to the path and towards the barn, her gaze to the building, feeling unsettled and apprehensive.

'What do he look like?' she asked as Clara's grip remained firm and their linkage forced her pace despite her wish to receive greater explanation before passing within.

'I done told you, he be a man of shadows and he stitched the back of Rosie's dress.'

They reached the doors and Lizbet finally dug her heels in, bringing them to a halt as her daughter reached for them. 'I ain't going in until you be telling me more.'

Clara turned to her with a desperate look. 'There ain't any time to be wasting,' she said. 'If you be making him better he can help with the harvest.'

She released her grip, passing through the left-hand door and into the gloom. Lizbet stood, held motionless by indecision and her mind filled with confusion.

'Ma, you must hurry,' called Clara as she went to the ladder.

Breaking the hold of her puzzlement, Lizbet stepped into the barn and looked around, her pulse increasing and feeling ill at ease. She walked over to the ladder as her daughter climbed up, turning her gaze to the hayloft above and feeling a warning within.

'Clara!' she called.

Her daughter paused near the top of the ladder. 'What?'

'It may be we should fetch help before we approach this... man.'

'He languishes and we must hurry,' she replied, vanishing from sight and her feet padding on the floorboards.

Lizbet stared up a moment and then followed after, her stomach churning. Her head rose over the side and she spied her daughter crouched in the shadows of the left corner. Looking beyond the girl, she spied a figure lying upon the straw in the growing brightness of the new day and her eyes widened as she stepped from the ladder.

'A nigger!' she exclaimed as she began to make her way over, bent at the waist to avoid hitting her head against the beams.

'Nigger?' asked Clara, looking questioningly over her shoulder.

'That be the name for his kind,' said Lizbet as she came to a stop just shy of her daughter, the last two words spoken with disdain.

'You done seen the likes of him before?'

She nodded. 'A plenty,' she replied. 'That ain't no man of shadows, that be a negruh, a man of dark skin.'

'Be there women too?'

Lizbet gave another nod of response, looking upon his prone form with a sour expression. 'He probably done runaway from his Master.'

Clara stared at her in bewilderment. 'Master?'

'We must let the authorities know he be abiding here.'

'You won't help him?' asked Clara in surprise.

'I ain't wasting time on tending no negruh. We need to be attending to the harvest, not to a no good slave,' she replied. 'Come. You set to the sweeping and I'll go fetch someone to take him away.' She turned and began towards the ladder.

'You can't just be leaving him like this.' The horror of Clara's tone brought her mother's steps to a halt.

Lizbet looked back at her daughter. 'He ain't mine and so I ain't got no cause to be helping him.'

'What you meaning, he ain't yours?'

'He be a slave, Clara,' she explained. 'He belongs to someone else and I ain't meddling with their property.'

'Property?' Clara glanced at Joshua. 'How can someone be property?'

'His kind be nothing more than dumb animals born to serve. They be sold like cattle at market.'

She looked at her mother in disbelief. 'Truly?'

Lizbet nodded again. 'So, you see, he ain't ours to be seeing to.'

Clara glanced to the boards as she thought on what had been said. 'But he abides in our barn,' she stated, raising her gaze once again. 'Maybe he ain't no one's property.'

Lizbet shook her head. 'There ain't no free negruh's in these parts. He's done runaway from where he belongs,' she explained. 'He still be someone else's property, like a cow that's done broken out of its enclosure. Like that cow, he needs to go back to where he belongs.'

Turning to Joshua, Clara remained crouched beside him as she studied his tormented expression. 'It ain't right,' she said miserably. 'He be a man, just like Pa.'

'Pa ain't no negro,' responded Lizbet, her tone hardening.

'What difference do that make? He still be a man.'

Lizbet saw the determined look in her daughter's eyes and knew there would be no persuading her to leave the negro be. It was underpinned by a feeling of mortification in response to what she'd said, one that wouldn't have been apparent if she'd paid more attention to teaching Clara the ways of the world.

She sighed and walked back to her side. Crouching, she reached forward and tentatively placed the backs of her fingers to the slave's forehead, feeling the burning of his skin beneath as she grimaced with the damp touch.

Lizbet put her hands to his far shoulder and rolled him onto his front with a tug of effort, both she and Clara shuffling backward a little. His vest was matted with blood and perspiration. It was stuck to his back in sickening ridges that hinted at what lay beneath.

'What happened to him?' asked Clara in whispered alarm.

'He were flogged.'

'Flogged?' She looked to her mother, swallowing against a wave of nausea.

'Given lashes with a whip for some crime he done committed,' answered Lizbet. 'You didn't know?'

Clara shook her head.

'It could've been punishment for some foul deed. You done put yourself in danger by associating with him,' she reprimanded. 'How long have you known he be hiding here?'

Clara's cheeks flushed with guilt. 'A day.'

'Why didn't you tell me?'

'He made me promise,' she replied, 'and I found no cause to think him anything but a kindly man.'

Lizbet frowned and shook her head. 'You've no idea what he did to deserve the whip. It could be he would have caused you harm had his health permitted.'

'Joshua wouldn't have hurt me,' she responded.

'You be young and naïve,' said Lizbet with a touch of regret. The sheltered existence on the farmstead had seemed idyllic, but that idyll had been broken by Walter's departure and now its limitations were further revealed.

'He wouldn't have done no harm to me,' insisted Clara.

Lizbet blinked away the brief recollection of lying with Walter in the grasses where the house now stood. 'You know no such thing.'

'If you won't treat him, then I be doing so,' said Clara, turning away from her mother and looking upon Joshua.

Lizbet thought about taking her daughter's hand and forcing her to withdraw from the slave, but hadn't the strength to do so, the disheartening sight of the flattened crop leaving her with no will to fight. 'I'll tend him,' she conceded.

Clara looked back to her in delight.

'But I'll also be paying Tyler a visit in the coming days to seek his advice and to find if he has heard tell of a runaway.'

Her daughter's expression fell.

'That be my offer,' she stated.

Clara nodded after pausing for thought. 'If you wait to visit, it may be Joshua can help bring in the harvest,' she said in an attempt at persuading her mother to delay her trip as long as possible.

'We shall see,' she replied, fully intending to leave within the next day or two. 'Now, fetch me a sharp knife and the rag used to clean the stove.'

'But that be dirty.'

'And that be the rag I'll use,' responded Lizbet. 'I won't be using good cloth on a nigger.'

Clara frowned, but rose to her feet and glanced at Joshua as he groaned. 'Do you think he will mend?'

'Hard to tell, but he has a better chance if you make haste,' she replied pointedly. 'And fetch one of your Pa's special bottles,' she added, referring to the unlabelled bottles of potato gin, Lizbet intending to use the alcohol to cleanse the negro's wounds.

Clara hesitated and then made her way to the ladder. Lizbet glanced over her shoulder to see her daughter's head pass below the level of the loft. She turned back to the slave and stared at the back of his vest.

'Tending a nigger,' she mumbled with a shake of her head, wondering if she'd made the right choice and pondering what crime had brought about such terrible punishment.

15

Lizbet pinched up the cloth at Joshua's shoulder and pushed the knife into its tautness. She began to run the blade down his back, having to tug the material from where it had stuck to the wounds. Clara grimaced at the sight of the deep cuts as the vest was cut and pulled away, yellow discharge glistening in the wounds.

'It smells bad,' she commented with a glance to her mother, pinching her nose shut.

Lizbet nodded. 'The wounds are infected.'

'Can you help him?'

'I can do my best,' she responded, trying to control a wave of nausea that came over her, the odour of the slave's faeces and urine also strong in the confines of the hayloft as she breathed through her mouth.

She peeled the shirt away from his lower back and let the two sides drop to the floor, feeling the dampness of sweat upon her fingers. Trying to push the feeling of disgust from her mind, Lizbet took up the blackened rag beside her and dipped it into the pail. Drops of dirty water fell as she lifted it, patting on the boards as she leant forward and began to clean the cuts.

Clara breathed deeply. 'I feel sick.'

Lizbet turned to find her daughter cradling her stomach. 'You have no need to attend.'

'I want to be of help.'

'Do you know the look of mustard root?' she asked as she rinsed the rag in the water.

'Yes.'

'Then you can be making yourself of use by finding some for me. It will help to fight the infection.' She leant forward and continued to cleanse the furrows left by the whip, the water darkening the floorboards.

'Before you leave, clear the straw from about his body,' she instructed as her daughter rose. 'He's already soiled a plenty.'

Clara moved to the far side of Joshua, forced low by the slant of the roof. She began to sweep the straw towards the opposite corner with her feet, careful not to let the soles rub on the boards for fear of splinters.

Lizbet took the knife to the braces lying loose beside the slave's britches. Readying herself to remove the leggings, she glanced over at her daughter as a realisation struck her. 'He done had the remainder of the stew,' she stated.

Clara blushed and nodded. 'I didn't want to lie,' she said, turning her gaze downward as she continued to corral the straw.

Lizbet frowned at her daughter and considered chastising her for the deception, but could see that she already chastised herself. She changed position and pulled at the britches with jaw set. She wriggled them down Joshua's legs and they came free with a jolt that sent her back, her backside thumping onto the boards. Dropping them in a heap with a look of disgust, she began to clean the slave of his soilings.

'Could you be fetching more water before the mustard root?' she asked.

Clara gave a nod and finished her task. She stepped over Joshua's feet and went to the ladder.

'The ground beneath the loft will be in want of a clean when I'm done. That be another task you can perform as thanks for my efforts,' said Lizbet over her shoulder as her daughter began to descend.

Turning her attention back to the cleansing, she wrung out the cloth and continued down his legs, hearing the faint patter of water on the ground below the loft. Joshua's build was similar to Walter's and her thoughts turned to her husband, gladly retreating from the negro she was confronted with.

She remembered when they'd lit the first fire in the hearth and cuddled before it beneath the patchwork blanket given by her mother, the construction of the cottage all but complete. It had been a time of contentment and their joy was soon added to by the blessing of being with child.

Lizbet rinsed the cloth and her gaze turned to the injuries upon the slave's back. She hoped that Walter fared well and asked God to watch over him when she said her nightly prayers. To find him returned badly injured or not returning at all would be a cross she did not think she could bare.

Joshua moaned, his cheek against the boards and mouth ajar, saliva hanging from his lips to the rough wood. She looked to his face and saw the pain. She imagined Walter's face wrought with similar agonies and tried to push the unwanted image from her mind.

The sound of Clara's entry into the barn drew her gaze over her shoulder. She listened as she climbed the steps, her progress measured as she hefted one of the buckets from the cottage to the hayloft.

'How goes it?' asked Clara as she spied her mother and took the last few steps.

'There be no change, but it'll take time for him to be making a recovery, if that be what he makes.'

Clara looked at her in alarm as she walked towards her, face showing the strain of carrying the pail. 'Do you think he could...?' She struggled to put voice to the last word, turning her gaze to Joshua as she came to a stop at her mother's side and lowered the pail to the floor.

Lizbet nodded. 'He be in a bad way and I ain't practised in medicine.'

'Should we fetch a doctor?' She crouched and looked at Joshua's tight expression.

'There ain't a one who'd treat a nigger.'

'But he suffers,' she responded indignantly.

'Suffering or no suffering, they ain't gonna be helping one of his kind.'

'You think that be right?' asked Clara, searching her mother's gaze.

Lizbet was careful how she phrased her reply. 'I think it be the way of things.'

'Then the way of things be wrong,' said Clara forcefully. 'There ain't no difference between him and Pa other than the colour of their skin.'

'That may be the all of it, but some say God Himself has made it so that the negro be servant and the white be master.'

'But you say God be fair and merciful.'

'God, not life,' responded Lizbet. 'That be how things are, Clara, and it ain't our place to be changing them. You be innocent of this world and time will bring you to understand.

'Now, if you want to be giving him every chance, you'd best be on your way and find some mustard root. I'll finish cleaning him and return to the house where I'll ready to make a poultice for his wounds.'

Clara frowned but voiced no further protest.

'Take the old water and be sure to tip it on the waste, we don't want the negruh's taint contaminating the crop or the crick,' said Lizbet, unstopping the bottle of potato gin that had been resting beside her.

'His name be Joshua,' said Clara, picking up the first pail.

She made her way to the ladder without saying another word, though her steps carried greater weight than before and her movements showed her dejection. Awkwardly passing down the ladder, she made her way out of the barn and into the sunlight. She felt its warmth on the back of her neck as she turned and made her way around the side of the building, confused and shocked by her mother's attitude, one that seemed out of place when set against the woman she thought she knew.

16

Lizbet placed the piece of cloth into the old and battered pan, the remedy within. She covered it in the thick balm, pushing it in with her knuckles so that the crushed roots would penetrate the fibres. 'You need to visit with him regularly to check on his condition and keep the poultice damp if need be,' she said over her shoulder.

Clara stood in the doorway, holding Rosie to her breast as she stared over at the barn, her impatience and worry clear to see in her restlessness. 'How much longer will it take?'

'Hurrying will not help, but hinder,' replied her mother with a reprimanding tone.

Clara looked over at her pleadingly.

'I'm almost done, but make sure to return without delay once you've done taken it out to him. Your chores will not see to themselves,' she said, not wanting her daughter to spend too much time with the slave and thereby create a greater attachment than was already evident.

'Will we be starting the harvest?' she asked, looking out to the corn, only a few ears having risen to greet the sun and large swathes still languishing after the passage of the storm.

'I'll check on the corn's readiness when I'm done with this,' replied Lizbet. 'Treating the negruh may prove costly when it comes to time that could have been spent reaping what we can.'

'Joshua,' stated Clara.

'His name be of no consequence,' she said, taking the cloth from the pan and turning to her daughter. 'It be like them rabbits, Clara. You mustn't get attached to the slave. When his master discovers his whereabouts...' She cut the sentence short before her tongue revealed what would be the likely outcome of the slave's discovery.

'What'll happen?' asked Clara nervously, sensing that her mother was trying to hide something which would disturb her.

'Don't be worrying yourself about it,' said Lizbet dismissively. 'Take this out to him and lay it over the wounds.' She stepped past the table and held out the cloth. 'Press it gently onto his back. Gently, mind.'

Clara took it, the mixture upon the cloth cool and slimy to the touch. She stared at it a moment and then raised her eyes to her mother's. 'What'll happen?' she asked again, her voice barely a whisper.

Lizbet regarded her a moment and then took a breath as she sought words that would not cause undue distress. 'His life may be taken,' she admitted, falling short of mentioning the noose that would likely be hung from one of the trees.

'They would kill him!' she exclaimed in horror.

'He be a runaway, Clara,' she responded. 'He be punished for some wrongdoing and then has tried to flee. He done sealed his own fate.'

'Maybe we can unseal it,' she said. 'If we say he caused no harm and mended Rosie, that may go in his favour.'

Lizbet shook her head. 'We don't know what he did to deserve the lashes. It could be he done something that no amount of good deeds will undo,' she said, 'or that his master will see his attempt at running as reason enough to bring about his end.'

'I'd run away if someone be treating me that way,' said Clara miserably.

'Then thank the Good Lord you won't be treated so. Now, get yourself to the barn,' she instructed, wishing to bring the conversation to an end. 'We've already wasted a good portion of the morning and it'd be wise not to waste anymore.'

'Shouldn't we bring him into the house?'

Lizbet's eyebrows rose in response to the question. 'Ain't no nigger coming in my house. 'Sides, how would we transport him from the loft?'

'But…'

'The barn's the best place for him,' added Lizbet, cutting off her daughter's protest, 'and you should be thankful I'm treating the negruh at all.'

Clara held her mother's stern gaze for a moment and then bowed her head. She made her way out of the cottage with stooped shoulders, pausing on the porch to survey South Field.

Walking along the path to the barn, she heard a woodpecker in the trees behind the building. She looked for its black and white feathers as the sound of its drumming mingled with the whisper of leaves in the gentle breeze, but could not discern its whereabouts.

Entering the barn, she went up to the hayloft, her expression tightening as she drew close to the top of the ladder. The view of the loft was revealed as she made the final steps and her gaze went to Joshua's sorry form. Her mother had left him upon his side facing the rear wall, his back bared to the interior and a jarring sight as she stepped up onto the boards.

Bowed and filled with disgust that someone should be beaten in such a way, Clara went to him. 'Joshua?' she said softly, hoping for a response, but receiving none.

'I've brung a poultice that'll help you to heal,' she stated, taking the edges of the cloth in her hands and pulling it wide in preparation to lay it on the gory wounds.

With a fortifying breath, she pressed the poultice to the cuts, feeling the ridges beneath her palms. Joshua moaned in response to the touch.

'Sorry,' she said regretfully. 'It cannot be helped,' she added as she continued to press it to his back until she was certain the balm held it in place.

Clara tentatively removed her hands and the cloth remained, only the top-left corner peeling back slightly. She reattached it and gently pushed on his uppermost shoulder to angle his back towards the roof so the poultice would stay in place.

Her hand slick with the curative, she sat on her haunches and stared at the back of his head, his black hair glistening with perspiration and neck ingrained with dirt which her mother had not washed away. She glanced to the pail beside her, the stained rag hung over its side.

She took it up and dipped it into the cool water, wringing it and then taking it to Joshua's hot skin. With circular motions, she gently rubbed away the grime as she hummed her song for Rosie. The tune lifted to the shingles, a dream of innocence now stolen.

She finished the song and withdrew her hand, her eyes filled with sadness. 'I must be leaving, but I'll return later,' she said, briefly laying her hand on the back of his head.

Clara rinsed out the rag and then washed the balm from her hands before rising. Making her way back down the ladder, she went to Elsa's cage and peered in, wishing to find some distraction from her melancholy. She put her palm to the wire and wiggled a finger through one of the holes as the rabbit sat on the straw and watched.

'Hello, Elsa,' she said. 'Be the fresh bedding to your liking?'

She looked to the water trough and saw that it was nearly empty. 'I'll fetch more when I can, along with some food,' she stated, 'and maybe later I'll be done with my chores and have time to pet you a little.'

She took her hand from the wire and watched a moment before heading towards the doors. Passing out of the barn, she saw her mother's bent form amidst the corn of South Field and wandered over to the edge of the crop.

'How do it look?' she called.

'Not ready,' stated Lizbet flatly as she straightened, rubbing an ear of corn between her fingers and letting the damp grains fall to her feet.

'More sun be needed as yet,' she said as she began to wade out of the field towards Clara, 'but I fear the damp will lay claim to at least a third of the crop.'

She stepped onto the grass and turned to look out over the dishevelled corn. 'The night dew will see to it that mildew sets in.'

'Be there no way to begin the reaping now?'

Lizbet shook her head. 'The grain would only rot in the sacks.'

'So what can we do?'

'Wait and pray the Good Lord shows us mercy.'

They both looked at the crop for a while as a pair of crows flew low over the field, cawing and crying as they made their way towards the creek.

'What chores would you have me do?' asked Clara, turning to her mother and seeing her concern. The corn was their main means of support and without a full harvest they would fall short of what they needed in order to see the winter through.

'There are bowls and the like that be in need of cleaning,' she replied without turning, 'and the goat be in need of milking.'

Clara stared at her profile for a moment and then took hold of her hand, the contact causing Lizbet to look down at her. 'Do not fret, Ma,' she reassured. 'All will be well.'

Lizbet nodded and squeezed her hand, but could offer no words to confirm her daughter's statement.

'When the dishes are done, you can be spending time with Elsa if that be your wish,' she said finally, using her daughter's name for the rabbit and forcing a thin smile. 'I'll set about the milking.'

'Won't you be needing my help? I could sweep the house out or beat the linens on the line.'

Lizbet shook her head. 'The activity will be a welcome distraction,' she said, not having to explain further as she glanced at the corn, 'but mind it be time spent with the rabbit and not the slave.'

They both turned back to the field. Their hands remained interlocked and the grip was tight as they both considered the possibility of a lean winter ahead.

17

Clara knelt at the edge of The Eddy and dipped the pail into the water, filling it halfway. Straining, she lifted it out onto the mudflat beside her and looked upstream, the sun glimmering on the waters. Two days had passed since her mother had begun to treat Joshua, but there had been no change in his condition. She had been hopeful of signs of recovery, but none had made themselves apparent. His skin still perspired and burned, his face losing some of its colour.

Sighing, she straightened upon the bank and picked up the pail. The water splashed within as she turned and stepped up onto the higher level of parched earth, feeling the cracks against the soles of her feet as the breeze rippled her blue dress.

Clara passed along the path and through the gate, glancing down the wide track that led south. The brief hope of seeing her father was vanquished by the trail's emptiness, the air above distorted by the heat of the day.

She made her way past the chopping block, walking along the front of the house on her way to the barn. Looked to the corn, she saw that a little more had risen, but the majority laid low and was beginning to brown.

Stepping into the barn, she was grateful for the shade it provided and paused to dip her hand in the water, running it across her brow. Moving to the ladder, she made her way up and found Joshua lying upon his front, his condition accompanied by moans and occasional movement.

Clara placed the bucket on the boards and looked to the poultice cloth upon his back. It had drawn less discharge from his injuries than on previous visits and she hoped it was a sign of improvement.

Crouching, she took up the rag that was lying on the floor, plucking a small strand of straw from the material. Wetting it, she held it over the cloth covering his back and dripped water onto the poultice, averting her gaze from the bonds that her mother had tied about his wrists and ankles the previous day. She had protested, but it had been to no avail. Her mother scolded her for being too trusting and said that when he woke there would be no taking flight.

Her expression tightened as she recalled seeing her mother burning the remains of Joshua's shirt. She would not take it into the house, but had placed it on the end of a stick and set light to the stained cloth near the waste heap, holding it at arm's length over the pile of excrement and vegetable peelings.

It was clear that she held Joshua in low regard and Clara had asked what cause she had to do so. Lizbet had responded with unkind words about negroes. When she pointed out that her mother had no cause to take against him personally other than the brush with which she tarred all his kind, she was reprimanded once again.

Joshua groaned as he lay before her and Clara's hand stilled on its way to wet the rag again. She waited, hoping to see his eyes open or to hear his voice.

There were no further signs of life.

She frowned and dipped the rag before squeezing it over his back, grateful that the cloth concealed his wounds. Hearing the sound of her mother entering the barn, she did not turn, but knew what she was coming to tell her.

'I'll be leaving now,' called Lizbet from below.

Clara didn't respond, but sat miserably with arms lowered to her sides as she stared at Joshua's face.

'Clara?'

'I be hearing you,' she responded snappily.

'Then make a reply when I speak,' scolded Lizbet with equal heat.

Clara looked over her shoulder and stuck out her tongue, a look of distaste upon her face which was hidden by her elevation in the hayloft.

There was a moment of silence.

'I'll be seeing you when I return, and don't be spending all your time with the slave. The sweeping has yet to be done.'

'I'm tending his wounds,' said Clara indignantly.

'And then you'll be attending to your chores,' replied Lizbet as she stared up at the hayloft.

Clara didn't offer a reply, unhappy that her mother still insisted on visiting with Tyler to inform him of Joshua's presence. She had tried to argue against the course of action, but there was no changing her mind.

Lizbet continued to look up for a moment and then turned. She made her way to the doors and exited the barn into the sunlight.

Beginning along the path back to the house, her steps faltered when she heard the sound of horse's hooves. Her pulse increasing, she looked out over South Field, gaze fixed on where the track passed through the trees beyond the far corner of the crop.

Seeing no clue as to who approached, Lizbet hurried to where the track began on the far side of the field. Her pace quickened by hopefulness, she looked south with wide eyes and discovered two soldiers clothed in grey making their way towards the farmstead, one slightly ahead of the other.

Narrowing her gaze and sheltering her eyes with a hand, she tried to make out their faces, but couldn't discern their features due to the brightness of the day. She took a couple of steps forward, filled with anticipation as she bit back the urge to call out Walter's name.

The soldier's faces gained clarity and her heart sank. They were young men, the one trailing no more than a boy in uniform. Her stomach churned as she backed away, a warning arising within.

Lizbet moved to the porch and stepped up, finding scant security in the presence of the house at her back. She stood before the open door and watched as they rode alongside the field of bedraggled corn, their pace ominously slow.

They passed around the corner of the field and turned towards her, plodding over to the front of the cottage.

'Be you Mrs Elizabeth Hill?' asked the lead soldier as he brought his horse to a halt.

She nodded, her stomach filled with nauseating lightness.

'I'm Lieutenant Clifton,' he introduced, touching the brim of his hat as it rested on his white-blonde hair, the down of early adulthood upon his upper lip. 'I'm afraid I have bad news,' he stated, holding his hand out to the private behind him.

The fresh-faced soldier opened the satchel hung at his hip and leafed through the bulging contents before withdrawing a folded piece of paper. He passed it to his superior, his expression one of weary resignation.

Clifton leant forward and held the paper out towards Lizbet. She stared at it, but remained steadfast upon the porch.

'He be dead?' she whispered.

The lieutenant nodded, straightening when it became apparent she would not take the note. 'I'm afraid so.'

'In battle?' She held him in her wide eyes, battling with the churning of her stomach and feeling faint.

Clifton regarded her a moment. 'If I have your leave?' he asked, raising the note.

She nodded her response, throat constricted and mouth running dry.

He unfolded the paper with what seemed like tortuous slowness, the sound causing shivers to pass through her as she watched.

The lieutenant looked to the note. 'He passed a month ago from malaria,' he stated flatly, lifting his gaze as he folded it back up.

'Malaria,' she echoed in a whisper.

Clifton nodded. 'A month ago.'

Lizbet stared past him, looking toward the empty track as her mind reeled. Walter was gone, had been taken not by bullet or cannon fire, but by sickness. She felt shock and a deep sense of loss. More than that, she felt a pang of profound disappointment. It was an ache that pained her to the core of her being. She had not sensed his parting, could recall no feeling of loss coming over her, and yet had felt sure that if he passed she would know it. Their bond had been strong and she'd thought it bound them no matter the distance between them.

'Ma'am?'

She blinked and turned back to him. 'I beg your pardon.'

'I said, we have other duties to discharge,' he stated, holding out the note once again.

She stared at the paper and then stepped from the porch on weak legs, stumbling slightly. Reaching up, she took the note from his grasp with quivering fingers.

'Much obliged,' he said, touching the brim of his hat and taking up the reins.

The young lieutenant nudged the horse in its flanks and gave a tug with his right hand, the mount turning. His companion followed suit and they began back along the track at a slow trot, the rear horse swishing its tail and whinnying briefly.

Clara watched through a gap in the slats of the barn wall as her mother swooned and slowly fell to her knees, the soldiers moving out of sight through the strand of trees to the south. She hastened to the doors and passed outside, running along the path to the house.

She pulled up shy of her mother, her heart racing. Lizbet was hunched over, one arm cradling her stomach and her mouth stretched wide. No sound issued from her depths as she rocked back and forth, looking to the sky with tormented eyes.

Clara stared at her, the sight unsettling and filling her with fear as she glanced at the note crumpled in her mother's tight grasp. She stood rooted to the spot by the spectacle of her mother's grief, held in place by the power of the raw emotion and in no doubt as to its cause.

A high and haunting wail suddenly burst from her mother's lips, forced from her by the tightness of her chest and cramp of her stomach. Her eyes were closed and her face to the sky as the tendons in her neck went rigid with the strength of the outpouring.

Clara stepped back as startled sparrows lifted from the corn. Tears sprang into her eyes and she began to weep in fear.

Her breath exhaled in heartfelt agony, Lizbet filled her lungs as if drowning. She began to weep, covering her face and drawing into herself as she sat upon the patchy grass.

'Ma?' Clara looked down upon her mother, catching her breath between sobs and face awash with tears.

Lizbet didn't respond, lost to her sorrow.

'Ma?' The word was filled with anxiety and pleaded for a response.

None came bar the continued sound of weeping.

'Be Pa...?' Clara couldn't bring herself to end the question as her body trembled.

Lizbet managed to nod, briefly looking up at her daughter, her eyes possessed with a desolation that sent a shivering bolt through Clara. The hairs on her forearms and at the nape of her neck tingled in response to the sight and the knowledge that her father would not return.

Her mother bowed her head once again and rocked as tears continued to fall, darkening the lap of her dress as mucus streamed from her nose. Clara watched for a few moments and then willed herself to her mother's side.

Crouching, she put her arm about her shoulders. Lizbet turned and gathered Clara to her, holding her with breathless tightness. They held each other with great need, their bodies wracked by sobbing as crows called in the trees beyond the corn and crickets sounded in the long grasses by the boundary fence.

18

'Pa said one day we'd have a ranch and I'd be having a horse of my own,' said Clara as she dripped water onto the cloth upon Joshua's back, her eyes sparkling with tears. 'I used to ride with him before he done went off to the war. Now I just be riding Bella when she pulls the plough.'

She dipped the rag into the pail beside her as she sat cross-legged before the slave, Rosie tucked into the cord about the waist of her faded red dress. 'He promised to take me to the capital when the war were over.'

She sighed and squeezed the rag above the covered wounds, watching the droplets fall.

'Washington.'

Clara went still in response to the whispered word. She looked to Joshua's face, his right cheek against the boards and a short tight beard having grown during his infirmity. His eyes were narrowly open as he regarded her.

She slowly shook her head. 'Richmond, Virginia,' she replied, barely believing him to be awake. 'How be you feeling?'

'Achy,' he replied hoarsely. 'Heavy,' he added after a moment.

'Me and Ma have done nursed you these last few days,' she informed him. 'The wounds on your back were infected.'

Joshua managed a vague nod, feeling the roughness of the wood against his cheek. 'Water.'

She looked to the contents of the pail, the water's discolouration highlighted by a diffused sliver of sunlight slanting in through a gap in the shingles, the sun hanging in the western sky. 'I'll fetch some,' she stated, beginning to rise.

'Stay,' said Joshua, trying to reach out to her, but finding his hands bound.

His brow creased and he looked down, his right arm trapped beneath the weight of his body and bound hands beside him.

Clara looked to the bonds regretfully. 'Ma done it,' she stated. 'She be set to thinking you'd run if given the chance.'

Joshua returned his gaze to her, blinking to clear his vision, his mind sluggish and disturbed by the aching that filled his body. His cheekbone was painful against the boards and he struggled to move onto his side to alleviate the pressure, finding the effort too much.

Clara rested the rag over the side of the pail and got to her knees. Taking hold of his near shoulder, she helped him change position, a moan of pain forced from him before he settled.

Checking that the cloth remained in place on his wounds, Clara rested back. 'I'll be fetching some water now,' she stated, rising to her feet. 'I shan't be long.'

She turned and hurried to the ladder. Descending to the floor, she soon exited the barn and made her way to the cottage. Walking through the open front door, she found her mother seated at the table with her back to the open shutters of the window. She'd been there since they'd risen from their embrace, remaining still and silent as she stared bleakly at the grain of the wood before her.

Clara moved to stand on the far side of the table. 'Joshua has woken,' she announced.

Lizbet did not respond.

'Ma?'

Her gaze remained fixed on the tabletop.

'Ma!' she exclaimed with greater force.

Lizbet raised her head, her gaze bringing to mind the howling of winter winds.

'Joshua has regained his own mind,' she said. 'Your nursing has done saved his life,' she added, hoping the knowledge would bring some little comfort and glad for the distraction from her own grief.

Lizbet shook her head miserably. 'The life of a no-good negruh is no fair trade for the life of your Pa,' she responded, lowering her gaze. 'No fair trade.' She shook her head.

Clara stared at her for a moment, her heart aching. Wishing to hide from the sadness that sought her out, she turned to the cups resting on the shelf in the corner near the stove-side cabinet. Stepping over, she took one down and filled it in the pail on the floor, the faint light reflected on the water's surface caught in the glistening of her eyes.

'I'll be taking this back out to him,' she stated, making for the doorway.

Lizbet didn't respond, sunk in the depths of her loss.

Clara hesitated and then passed out onto the porch, making her way back along the path to the barn while blinking away her tears. She went to the hayloft and looked to Joshua's face as she approached his naked form, finding that his eyes had closed.

'Joshua?' she whispered as she crouched beside him.

His eyes flickered open and she held the cup out before them. He tried to rise on his arm, but was too weak as yet.

Clara put the cup down briefly as she moved forward and cradled his head in her hand. Taking it up again, she placed it to his lips and tipped a little of the liquid into his mouth. Joshua drank with his eyes closed as she continued to tip with small increments.

Keeping his lips closed when his thirst was quenched, Clara lowered his head back to the boards. Putting the cup aside, she saw there was only a small wash left in the bottom.

He looked to her and studied her face for a moment. 'There be something greater troubling you than my sorry state,' he croaked, licking his lips.

She turned her gaze to the floor between them, focussing on a stray piece of straw lying forlornly on the rough wood. 'Pa ain't going to be coming back from the war,' she stated, her tone and expression saying what she could not.

'I'm sorry that be so,' he responded after a pause, wincing as he shifted position slightly.

She nodded sadly, keeping her gaze to the solitary stem, its gold darkening with rot. 'I miss him,' she said softly, her eyes welling in response to the admission. 'Be your parents alive?' Clara lifted her gaze to his.

He stared at her a moment before responding. 'I don't know.'

'You don't know?' She looked at him in surprise, wiping a stray tear from her cheek.

Joshua shook his head. 'I ain't done seen them since soon after we reached St Louis,' he replied, coughing momentarily.

'Did your parents be losing you there?'

'They didn't go losing me,' he said with a vague shake of his head. 'We was taken to a slave pen, but us children was moved to another after a few days. I were sold separate from my Ma and Pa.'

Clara stared at him, unable to fathom how people could be bought and sold, the concept alien to her experience. 'How old was you?'

'Abouts your age.'

She looked at him in shock. 'You've been a slave nearly all your life?'

He managed a weak nod. 'It be seventeen years since I were done taken from Africa.'

'Africa?'

'A long ways from here,' he explained, 'more miles than you can count. It were home, but only be a half-remembered dream now.'

'Can't you go back.'

'There ain't no going back,' he said sadly, the conversation starting to sap his energy.

'Maybe me and Ma can...'

'There ain't no going back,' Joshua repeated firmly as he held her gaze. 'There be only one way a slave leaves this country,' he added darkly.

Her expression became pinched in response to the implication of his words and the loss of her father was brought back into focus. 'Not just slaves,' she said beneath the weight of his dark eyes.

Joshua softened, a yawn forcing itself upon him as weariness began to draw his lids down. 'I don't mean to offend.'

'You didn't offend,' she replied, glancing at him before reaching for the length of straw and toying with it. 'Does the loss get easier to bear?' Her voice was soft and her tone hopeful of solace.

'It be a cross upon your back the rest of your days,' he said, Clara looking at him in mild alarm, 'but it be a weight that lessens with passing years.'

He yawned again as the strand snapped and she stared down at the sorry pieces, releasing them and letting them tumble to the boards.

'I should be leaving you to rest,' she said, shifting in readiness to rise. 'I'll return with food after supper.'

Joshua gave a nod as she picked up the cup and got to her feet.

'I'll bring more water,' she added, holding up the cup.

She started towards the ladder and then came to a halt, looking back at him as he lay in the gathering shadows. 'It be good to see you recovering, Joshua,' she stated before continuing to make her way back to the cottage.

19

Clara walked into the house to find her mother still seated at the table, her arms resting on the top and shoulders slumped. The stove was unlit and Lizbet had made no supper.

She moved over to the pail in the far corner. 'I spoke with Joshua,' she stated as she passed around the table.

'Clean the cup at The Eddy,' instructed her mother flatly.

Clara glanced at the cup in her hand before turning to her mother. 'Can't I just rinse it here? He only be having water.'

'It must be scrubbed after the negruh has used it.'

Her expression tightened, but she voiced no complaint. Stepping to the table, she went to put the cup on its surface.

'Outside,' stated her mother, looking at her coldly.

'But...'

'No buts, Clara. Put the cup outside beyond the porch. I'll not have his taint inside.'

She could tell by her mother's tone that there was no point in argument and had no wish to bandy words with her after the news that had been delivered that day. Turning, she made her way back out of the house and stepped off the porch, bending to place the cup upon the earth near the chopping block.

Returning and moving to face her mother and the open window beyond, she took hold of the back of the chair before her. 'You want I should make supper?'

Lizbet didn't respond.

'I could be making a broth with vegetables and cuts from the leg of mutton,' she suggested.

'I've no appetite, though it seems yours ain't been affected.' There was accusation in her tone.

Clara detected the rebuke and her brow creased. 'I'll make it and maybe the smell of the cooking will wake your belly.'

'And there'll be three portions, no doubt,' said Lizbet bitterly.

Clara made no reply, sensing that to do so would only rile her mother, who seemed like a coiled spring filled with tension. She turned to the simple stove and opened the soot-blackened door. She proceeded to place kindling inside, taking it from a large and roughly woven basket that had seen better days, its weave broken in places and thick with cobwebs at the sides as it rested on the floor in the corner of the room.

Taking a few small pieces of timber from the woodpile resting between the basket and chimney, she placed them atop the kindling. She retrieved the matches from the shelf above and crouched before the open stove. Striking one against the roughness of the cabinet to her right, she moved its flickering flame to the twigs, watching as it took and began to greedily devour what was offered to its consumption.

She walked into the hallway and stepped inside the pantry. Going to the sacks along the wall, she took out a selection of root vegetables, cradling them against her. She reached up and took hold of the leg of mutton, lifting it so as to unhook its hanging cord from the ceiling while keeping her gaze averted from the rabbit carcasses beyond.

Returning to the main room, Clara placed the ingredients on the tabletop before fetching the chopping knife and board. She proceeded to slice the vegetables, the tap of the blade upon the wood filling the evening hush. Slivers of mutton followed, its toughness causing her to cut with a sawing motion.

Once finished, she took the leg back to the pantry, having need of a wooden step that her father had made in order to re-hang it. She paused in the cool darkness, staring at the half-empty sack of potatoes below the meat. The image of her father pulling up the potato plants came to mind as she followed after and helped to gather the crop into sacks. He'd begun to whistle her song for Rosie, encouraging her to sing along as they worked, adding jaunty melodies between the repeated verses.

Taking a wavering breath, Clara turned and went back to the main room. Going to the stove, she looked into the cooking pot. Seeing there was no water within, she picked up the pail by her feet and emptied some of the contents into it, her arms and shoulders straining beneath the weight.

Stoking the fire and holding her palm over the stove, she felt the first trace of heat beginning to rise. She took the pot to the table and swept the vegetables and mutton into it before setting it back on the growing warmth.

Taking the seat opposite her mother, she pulled Rosie from her waist. Holding the doll before her, elbows on the tabletop, she began to hum her tune and stroke her red woollen hair.

'Quiet!' snapped her mother, glaring over at her.

Clara looked up and then turned her gaze back to the doll. She turned Rosie around and ran her thumb over the rough mend that Joshua had made.

'I suppose you be happy the soldiers came by today.'

She raised her eyes again, looking at her mother in puzzlement.

'I still be fixing to visit with Tyler and tell him of the slave,' said Lizbet.

Clara realised the implication of her words and shock registered in her expression. 'I ain't happy they came by,' she said, her tone filled with hurt that her mother should think such of her.

Lizbet's eyebrows rose in obvious doubt. 'You seem unaffected by the news they done delivered,' she accused. 'Don't you care that Pa won't be a coming home?'

Clara was aghast and her eyes began to glisten. 'How can you be saying such a thing?'

'You have more care for the nigger than your Pa's passing.' Her mother's tone was laced with distaste.

She shook her head. 'That ain't true,' she pleaded, the first tears beginning to fall and Rosie trembling in her grasp.

Lizbet held her in an unforgiving stare.

'That ain't true,' she repeated with more force, trying to convince her mother.

There was no response bar the harshness of her mother's gaze, her narrowed eyes filled with heated accusation. The taut silence was oppressive, pressing in on Clara until she found it hard to take breath.

'It just ain't true,' she reiterated as she quickly stood.

Clara turned and ran from the room, sobbing uncontrollably as she padded down the hallway and went to the deepening gloom of her bedroom. She threw herself onto the cot and buried her face in the pillow. She wept into the hush, Rosie clutched to her chest but offering little comfort as the sun dipped below the horizon and night chased the last of its brightness into memory.

20

Clara opened the shutters of her bedroom window onto the new day. A thick bank of pale cloud laid low over the landscape. She looked to the trees ahead, the brush beyond visible between the trunks and a thin mist softening the scene. Her father had been intending to clear it in order to create a large north field, but had yet to take to the task before leaving for the war, only a small pasture having been planted with corn intended as chicken feed.

Feeling the prick of tears, she looked to the right, gaze following the course of the creek upstream. She could make out its mist-veiled waters here and there, between reeds or where the bank lowered with the rise and fall of the land. Its surface was steely grey in the dull light, unadorned by the sparkle of the sun as the clouds shrouded its presence.

She stepped to the cot and took up Rosie from beside the pillow, cover messed and hinting at the disturbed night's sleep she'd endured. Tucking the doll at her waist, she noted the wrinkles in her dress. She'd cried herself to sleep, drained by the powerful emotions and failing to change into her nightgown.

Clara exited, stepping into the hallway and seeing that the front door was closed as she made her way to the main room. She came to a stop by the table, finding no sign of her mother. Glancing around, her gaze briefly lingered on the stilled hands of the grandmother clock standing by the wall behind the lounging chairs.

Looking over her shoulder, she peered at her mother's bedroom door and wondered if she could still be sleeping. She listened for any snore or snuffle, but heard nothing but the birds outside and the distant lowing of Bella. After a moment of indecision, she turned and went back along the hall.

She stood before the door and listened once again, still hearing no sounds of slumber. Knocking gently, she opened it and peered in. The shutters were open and the bed empty, her brow creasing as she wondered at her mother's whereabouts.

Making her way back to the main room, she went to the stove, finding the cooking pot still resting on top and the broth untouched within. She frowned as she looked at its thickness, the vegetables pallid and soft after being allowed to simmer too long.

There was a soft banging. She turned sharply to stare at the door before realising the sound was merely the breeze stirring the window shutters.

Clara padded around the table and opened them, peering out at South Field. The mist hung over the corn, thickening towards the creek and masking the boundary fence, its low timbers merely stripes of shadow within the paleness.

There was still no sign of her mother and a thought came to mind that caused her expression to stiffen. 'Maybe she's gone to Tyler's?' she whispered, her pulse increasing.

Clara looked around the room for any clue as to her mother's possible departure, but found none. 'She may be in the barn tending the rabbits,' she said in an attempt at self-reassurance, 'or opening the chicken coop.'

With quick steps, she made for the front door and passed out of the cottage. Her pace increased as she followed the path to the barn, her stomach churning at the thought of her mother revealing Joshua's presence to the tobacco chewing farmer.

Seeing the chicken run empty and the hatch in the coop still close, she rushed into the barn. Sounds of disturbance arose from the rabbit hutches in response to her entry as she glanced around with wide eyes, finding the interior empty.

'Ma?' she called, looking to the hayloft.

'She ain't up here.' Joshua's rasping response was punctuated by coughing.

Clara considered retreating in order to check the outhouse and east fields, but decided to visit with the slave beforehand. She hurried across the dusty floor and ascended the ladder, finding him leant against the wall in the corner.

She went to him and crouched. 'How goes it?' she enquired.

Joshua nodded. 'Better, but I be weak and in need of food,' he replied. 'You didn't return as you said you would.'

'I...' She struggled for an explanation. 'I weren't able,' she said, not wishing to divulge what had transpired between her and her mother.

'I'll be bringing you some shortly. I've chores to do first,' she stated.

Joshua nodded again, his continuing recovery apparent in his eyes, which shone with a renewed light, the whites with greater clarity as the infection retreated.

'Turn so I may see your back,' she instructed.

'It be without enough pain that I can rest against the wood,' he said, sitting forward with a slight wince and turning so she could see the cloth.

There were virtually no stains of blood or fluid upon the paleness and it seemed the healing was making good progress. She leant forward and peeled the uppermost corner back far enough to see the top of one of the wounds, finding it closed and without obvious sign of infection.

'How do it look?'

'Good,' she replied as she tried to put the corner back in place, but the cloth fell away from the skin. 'I need to wet it again.'

She moved to the pail and took up the rag, dipping it into the water with apparent haste.

'What agitates you?' he asked as she transported the dripping rag over his head and let the droplets fall upon the cloth.

She thought before answering, not wanting to alarm him with the truth. 'I've lots to be done,' she replied simply.

Clara concentrated her efforts on the sagging corner and stuck it back in place over his skin. 'There,' she stated, moving back from him and hanging the rag over the side of the pail once more. 'I must get to it, but I'll be returning with broth and bread as soon as I'm able.'

'I ain't going nowhere,' he responded, glancing at his bonds.

She followed his gaze and blushed, embarrassed by the bindings her mother had seen fit to tie in place. She turned and began to make for the ladder.

'Where be my clothes?' he called after her. 'It gets awful cold in nothing but my skin.'

Clara took hold of the ladder and turned to position herself upon the top rung. 'I'll fetch your britches with the food,' she replied, unsure what her mother had done with them.

'And my shirt?'

'I'll find something.' She moved down the ladder and walked quickly to the doors, checking that Rosie was secure at her waist. 'Where do you think she could be?'

she asked the doll as she stepped out into the still morning.

She stared to the right, the trees spectral in the thickening mist. There was a sensation of being watched as they stood shadowy and silent against the brightening clouds. Shivering momentarily, she went towards them, following the path to the east fields.

Scurrying arose from the undergrowth as she passed beneath the boughs, her pulse becoming elevated once again. A canopy of woodland hung in the distance like a dark cloud, low against the skyline, its lower reaches obscured by the mist and its sight giving rise to an ominous feeling as she broke from the strand.

Bella stood tethered in a stretch of thick grasses between the trees and a field of corn to the left. Another rested on the other side of the path and it was there that Clara's gaze settled upon a figure knelt within the crop and veiled in mist.

'Ma?' she called as she stepped to the edge of the field.

There was no movement from the bowed form of her mother as Clara's brow creased in puzzlement. A golden glow was cast about Lizbet, faint and diffused in the moist air. She could not discern is source and wondered at its meaning. Its vague aura seemed like the presence of God, surrounding her in His compassion, healing the pain that the world of men had wrought upon her.

Moving into the field, she made towards her mother. As she drew closer through the battered corn, she spied a lantern set upon the ground and thoughts of a holy presence vacated her.

She stopped a few yards short of Lizbet, unable to see her down-turned face. 'Ma?'

'We are undone,' she whispered.

Clara spied an ear of corn upon her mother's cupped hands as they rested on her lap. The grains were darkened and the white down of fungal growth was visible.

'Surely not all the crop be tainted,' she said, glancing around at the crumpled field. 'There'll be plenty that can be harvested.'

Lizbet shook her head. 'I haven't the strength,' she said in defeat. 'It may be best if we accept our lot and make a return to Jeff City.'

Clara looked at her in surprise. 'We've done faced hardship before.'

'Hardship, not ruin,' responded her mother, looking up and revealing the howling voids of her eyes, the shadows of sleeplessness accentuating her desolation.

Clara bit back her immediate response, worried that mentioning the prospect of Joshua being able to help bring in the harvest would agitate her mother. She glanced around in the hope of finding something to deviate the conversation, sure that her mother's grief was clouding her judgement, but that the clouds would pass.

'Why have you brung the lantern?' she asked, gaze settling upon its illumination.

Lizbet glanced at it and then looked back to her hands, head bowing once again. 'I couldn't sleep but a wink and came a wandering before daybreak,' she replied. 'Your Pa walked with me.'

'You saw him?' asked Clara, looking into the mist hanging over the field and longing to see him standing amidst the corn.

Her mother shook her head. 'I felt him beside me. He'd come to say farewell.'

Lizbet took a breath and returned her gaze to her daughter. 'The stars and moon were veiled. The mist were stirring with life and I knew it to be him,' she said with a haunted look. 'He were with me, Clara. He were with me and now he be gone until I join him through the gates from which there be no return.'

'He didn't visit with me,' she responded despondently.

'It may be he done visit while you slept, watching over you like he did so oft when you suffered from the whooping cough.'

Clara thought back to when she'd first woken, the faint smell of earth and potatoes rising from the floorboards. She couldn't recall sensing anything out of the ordinary and felt a pang of disappointment. 'I don't think he came to me.'

Lizbet reached out and took hold of her hand, the ear of corn falling to the ground. 'He did, I be sure of it,' she reassured, giving her hand a squeeze. 'You were the apple of his eye and he wouldn't have done parted this world without saying farewell to us both. It be a hap of chance that I were wakeful when he came to me.'

'You don't think he'll come again?' asked Clara, hoping her mother would offer some hope as to his return.

Lizbet shook her head. 'He done departed this world now. There ain't no coming back,' she said, her daughter's expression falling. 'Don't fret, Clara, we be seeing him again one fine day.'

Clara nodded as tears welled in her eyes. She would have given anything to sense her father's presence one last time, to feel him near and find comfort in his protective strength. She had always felt secure on the farmstead, her father a rock which gave her protection and a sense of solidity.

Lizbet got to her feet, keeping her grip on her daughter's hand. 'We best be breaking the fast,' she stated, her own eyes swollen with the waters that had yet to recede, her grief close.

She bent and fetched up the lantern, blowing out the flame that had been all but overpowered by the daylight.

Leading the way and pulling her daughter into motion, she took them from the field and back to the path. Bella lowed as they departed the eastern pastures, tears upon Clara's cheeks being cooled by the mist that stirred with their soft passage.

21

Reaching into the middle cage of those lining the barn floor, Clara withdrew the buck. Her hands around its body, she was careful to hold it away from her as its rear legs raked the air. She straightened and pushed the hutch door closed with her foot so the pregnant doe within would be unlikely to escape and then transferred the buck to one of the cages on the shelf. Fastening it closed, she glanced in to see the male rabbit already taking an interest, sniffing the prospective mate within.

With a deadpan expression, she went back to the lower cage and turned the nub of wood to secure the door. Straightening, she looked along the lines, satisfied that the bedding had been changed and they were all fed.

Clara went to the ladder and made her way to the hayloft. Joshua was seated in the corner with an empty bowl beside him. He'd hungrily tucked into the bread and broth after putting on his britches, which she'd cleaned at The Eddy after breakfasting with her mother. They'd been found in the empty stall below, a few maggots crawling on them and feeding on the residue of Joshua's body, their presence warranting the use of a stick to take them up and carry them to the creek.

'How you feeling?' she asked as she approached.

'Better for the food,' he replied. 'I'm much obliged to you, Miss Clara.'

She crouched before him and noted the darkness on the boards where he sat, the dampness of the britches seeping into the wood.

'They'll be drying in time,' he said with a thin smile as he noted the direction of her gaze.

Clara nodded and there was a brief silence.

'I be in need of the outhouse,' he said.

She turned her gaze towards the floor. 'The pail,' she stated.

Joshua looked to the half-full bucket of water resting beneath the eaves.

'Ma say she ain't having no nigger use the outhouse.' Her cheeks flushed.

He studied her a moment. 'Ain't no need for you to feel bad,' he stated.

'If it were down to me, you wouldn't be bound in rope or stuck out here in the barn,' she revealed, turning her gaze to his. 'Her treatment of you be beyond my comprehension, but she say it be the way of things.'

Joshua gave a nod, all trace of his smile having vanished. 'This world be that of the white folk.'

She looked into his eyes. 'Be you different in ways more than appearance?'

He shook his head. 'Not that I knows of.'

'Then I have no mind for this "way of things",' she stated.

'Then there be hope.'

She cocked her head in response to his words, studying him for a while. 'How be your strength?' she asked, her thoughts turning to the situation at hand.

'Much improved, but with much improvement as yet to make.'

'We be needing help with the harvest. A storm came through and done weathered the crop beyond repair.'

'A little more food be building my strength quicker,' he said with a glance to the bowl.

'You'll help?'

'Ain't never be asked do to anything for white folk before, only told.'

She looked at him in puzzlement, but he didn't expand.

'I reckons I'll be able to swing a scythe right soon, and it'll be fine to be out in the sun again.'

Clara's expression brightened. 'On the morrow?'

He couldn't help but chuckle in response. 'If able, Miss Clara,' he nodded. 'If able.'

'I'll be fetching more of the broth,' she stated, reaching for the bowl and then rising. 'I'll tell Ma that all ain't lost, thanks to you.'

Joshua watched as she made her way to the ladder and passed out of sight. His smile faded as he looked to the pail. Awkwardly reaching to the top of his back with his bound hands, he scratched at irritation beneath the cloth and it began to peel from his skin.

Pulling it away, he winced with mild pain and dropped it by the bucket. Twisting one way and then the other, he found little suffering in the movement.

'It may be on the morrow,' he said to himself with another nod before rising to relieve himself in the pail.

22

She took the stale last of the bread from the bin and placed the lid back on top. Taking up the bowl of broth from the cabinet, she turned for the door to find her mother standing there, the beaten field at her back. A small pile of washing rested in the basket she was holding and a pail hung from the crook of her arm with the washboard within.

'For the slave?' There was disapproval in her tone.

Clara nodded. 'For Joshua.'

'Ain't he had enough?'

'He needs to build his strength. He gonna be helping with the harvest,' she said, her words hopeful. 'I done asked him and he say that be fine.'

'You don't ask a negruh,' responded Lizbet with a shake of her head.

'We may yet get the harvest in.'

'What remains of it.' Lizbet placed the basket of damp clothes upon the table. 'Get these hung out before you set to molly-coddling the negruh.'

'I ain't molly-coddling him. I just be trying to help him mend.'

'Because he done mend your doll?' She snorted and shook her head again. 'You be soft-hearted, Clara, and that ain't always a good thing in this here world.'

'You done brung me up,' responded Clara defensively.

'And maybe I shouldn't have been sparing the rod. You need to toughen that skin of yours,' responded

Lizbet. 'I want you to kill the rabbits next time there be need.'

Clara paled. 'I can't.'

'You can and will,' stated her mother firmly, 'and you don't want to go getting attached to the nigger. He ain't gonna to be here long.'

'Be you going to Tyler's?' she asked with pulse rising.

Lizbet glanced out of the door at the crop. 'I'll be waiting until the harvest is done, but if his master comes looking I'll not conceal his presence here.'

'Even if they be wanting to kill him?'

Lizbet nodded. 'He be their property and they'll do what they will.'

Clara looked at her mother in dismay, unable to come to terms with the contrast between the woman she knew and the one who could be so callous when it came to Joshua's life.

'Now get to hanging the washing,' said Lizbet, looking to the floorboards, 'and you've yet to sweep the floors.'

'Can I take the broth before sweeping?'

'Chores come before some runaway negruh. The morning be nearly done and he can wait,' replied Lizbet sternly. 'Be that the last of the bread?' she asked, looking to the end in her daughter's hand.

Clara nodded.

'Then you can be putting it back in the bin.'

'I can be making more this afternoon. This be stale and riddled with mould.'

'You'll return it to the bin,' instructed Lizbet with a hard edge to her tone.

Clara hesitated and then placed the bowl and piece of bread on the tabletop. 'I'll bake more this afternoon,' she reiterated.

'I'll not be asking again.'

She looked at her mother with a pinched expression, unwilling to disobey and yet unwilling to place the bread back inside the bin. 'Joshua needs to build his strength if he be helping with harvest,' she said pleadingly. 'It best served to him. We can have fresh with supper this evening.'

'Clara.' Lizbet's tone was low and carried the threat of punishment.

She stood undecided for a moment longer and then swiped the bread from the table. Turning, she stepped to the bin and lifted the lid, placing the end inside before slamming the top back in the heat of her frustration.

Lizbet snatched up the broom from beside the door and moved around the table towards her with taut purpose. Clara turned and her expression dropped as she held up her hands and retreated into the corner, the basket of kindling against the back of her legs.

'I didn't mean to bang it,' she stated.

'Bend over and up with your dress.'

'I didn't mean it,' she protested again.

'I'll switch you where you stand if you don't be doing as you're told.'

Clara looked at her mother with begging eyes, but there was no forgiveness in her gaze, only the heat of anger. She moved away from the corner and bent over, raising the hem of her dress to reveal the back of her legs.

With practised swipes of the broom, Lizbet whipped the switches across her calves. Clara winced with each strike, the twigs stinging her skin hotly and raising tears to her eyes. Her mother struck her five times and a brief silence ensued.

'Now get to the hanging. I hear one more word of argument from you and there'll be more switching and no supper this evening.'

Clara let her dress fall back into place and straightened. She refused to look at her mother as she wiped the tears from her eyes and felt the smarting of the welters that had risen upon the backs of her legs. She took up the basket of washing, gritting her teeth against the urge to cry.

Walked quickly out of the cottage and around to the line, the passage of the air over her legs helped to calm the pain. She placing the basket on the grass and took up the first garment, hanging the dark overalls as she continued to struggle with her emotions.

A few smalls were next to be hung followed by her green dress, all hanging limp in the stillness of the day as the sun burned away the last of the mist, the bank of cloud having passed to the south. She glanced at the house as she hung one of her mother's shirts, hearing sounds of activity from the main room.

The last of the clothes placed over the line, she hesitated in returning to carry out the chore of sweeping. She had no wish to be in the presence of her mother, feared her dark mood would be lurking like a cougar in the brush, ready to pounce should she give the slightest opportunity.

'I wish I was like you,' she stated, looking down at Rosie. 'I wish I didn't feel,' she added, not only referring to the punishment that had been received, but also the bite of her mother's words and the loss of her father.

'Pa would have understood,' she said miserably as she took up the basket and began towards the front of the house with slow steps, Molly giving a bleat of farewell.

Walking into the main room, her shoulders hunched with tension, she found her mother stood before the table kneading dough in a large earthenware bowl.

'You shan't be needing to sweep for now, the dust will only get into the dough,' said Lizbet, her guilt at having struck her daughter serving to motivate her into the baking of a fresh loaf. 'Go take the broth to the negruh, but don't be lingering too long.'

Clara nodded, but voiced no comment. She took the bowl from the table with head bowed and then exited the cottage, grateful not to have received further reprimand.

Walking along the path to the barn, the heat of the day building and the grasshoppers chirruping within the grasses, she felt her tension lift. With the stinging of her calves as a reminder of her need not to take too much time with Joshua, she entered the building and passed inside.

23

Clara bent to pick up a small branch and added it to the timber already collected in the crook of her arm. She looked about the ground for more as she moved through the strand of trees north of the farmstead, the rear of the outhouse visible through the sparse trunks and the cottage beyond. Her face glistened with perspiration and she was thankful for the shade.

'Rosie, oh Rosie, my best friend,' she began to sing, the words not carrying the jaunty tone of previous renditions, but laced with sadness.

'Pull a stitch and he done mend,
As sweet as molasses, as warm as the sun...'

Her words trailed off as her gaze settled on the northern horizon. Rising above the brush and distant trees was a tower of dark smoke.

'A battle?' She asked the stillness as she paused in her task.

Clara listened for any hint of cannon fire, but heard only subdued birdsong and the sounds of insects that arose with the heat. She stared at the smoke a little longer and then turned her gaze back to the ground, spying a small branch a short distance ahead.

Gathering it up and feeling the strain in her shoulder, she began towards the cottage. She spied her mother beating out the rug that usually rested before the lounging chairs as it hung over the line, the washing having been cleared. Puffs of dust lifted with each hit and her mother's motions reminded her of the punishment that had been given that morning.

'Are you done with the firewood?' asked Lizbet as she noted her daughter's approach, lowering the beater as she peered over the sag in the line caused by the rug.

Clara nodded. 'This be my fifth load.'

'Ain't there a sixth to be had?'

She came to a stop before the line. 'My shoulder aches,' she responded as Molly bleated from where she was tethered beside the barn.

'It shows you been working,' responded Lizbet. 'If you ain't aching by the end of the days then you ain't been putting enough effort into them. That's what my Pa used to say.'

'I still have need to feed the rabbits and collect the eggs.'

'That can wait. Gather up some more while the light be good.'

Clara frowned and moved to the side, passing beneath the line and to the front of the cottage. She walked over to the chopping block, the timber she'd already collected piled between it and the porch in readiness to be sorted, the pieces small enough for the fireplace and stove to be taken in before the night's moisture took hold.

Dropping the lengths within her arms, she sighed and looked to her waist to check that Rosie remained secure. 'If only you could be lending a hand and not just your company,' she commented.

Passing back around the side of the house, she watched her mother strike the rug with vigour. 'There be smoke rising to the north,' she commented as she walked by and ducked despite the line's height being greater than her own.

Lizbet looked to the trees and saw the dark fumes between the trunks and boughs, her eyes narrowing as she stopped the beating.

'I thought it may be a battle, but done heard no cannon,' stated Clara without turning, continuing to walk towards the trees.

Lizbet stared at the smoke awhile, a shiver passing through her without apparent cause. She turned her gaze to the rug as she pondered the banner of smoke, wondering at its source and beginning the beating once more.

24

Her head lifted above the level of the floor and she looked to Joshua, finding him sleeping on his side and having gathered some of the remaining straw to use as a bed. His eyes opened as she stepped up onto the boards.

'Howdy,' he greeted, pushing himself up, his expression briefly tightening with pain.

'I have some supper,' stated Clara as she padded over to him with a bowl in hand. She had asked to take the stale end of the old loaf, but her mother had still refused despite having baked another.

She handed him the bowl and then seated herself before him. 'Rabbit stew,' she stated as he sniffed the lukewarm contents. 'The remainder from the pot.'

'Much obliged, Miss Clara,' he responded, lifting the bowl to this mouth and tipping it, hands cupped beneath.

Clara glanced at the rope which bound his wrists and then slipped Rosie from the cord about her waist. 'Her dress be made from one of Pa's old shirts,' she said as she stared at the doll.

'Mmm,' nodded Joshua before swallowing. 'She be a fine doll, for sure.'

'I like her hair.' She stroked Rosie's red locks. 'It be striking.'

Joshua raised the bowl again and took a large mouthful. Clara thoughtfully ran her thumb over Rosie's smile as she started to feel the chill of coming night creeping into the air.

'What do you reckon be after this life?' she asked, the question surprising Joshua as he chewed on a piece of meat.

He shrugged as he finished the mouthful. 'I reckon it don't really matter. We all gonna find out one way or another.'

'You don't think about it?'

Joshua shook his head. 'There ain't no point. This be where I am. Where I'm gonna be will come in good time whether I be a thinking about it or not.'

'What did your Ma and Pa say was after?'

'Heaven for good folk and hell for them that's not,' he stated before tipping the last of the stew into his mouth. 'If that be right,' he said through the food, 'then hell be a mighty full place.'

'My Pa's gone to heaven. I'll meet him there one day.'

Joshua swallowed the last of the meal. 'May that day be a good many years to come.'

'Amen,' said Clara with a gentle smile.

He chuckled and lowered the bowl to his lap. His expression of amusement faded as he looked to the rope about his ankles. 'It sure be hard to work with my legs bound. Do you think your Ma be letting me take off the ropes?'

She frowned and shook her head.

'It even gonna be hard getting down them there steps.'

'What did you do?' she asked softly after a few moments, wary of what his response may be.

'What be your meaning?' he responded.

'To earn the whipping. What crime did you commit?' She looked into his eyes, seeing no sign of malignance residing there.

'Master say I steal eggs, but I didn't.'

'You done earned the lashing for only stealing eggs?' she asked in shock.

122

'I didn't steal them. I done took two for Nettie.'

'Nettie?'

'She were another slave on Benedict Farm. She'd spent three days in The Stove and needed her strength building. If I didn't be feeding her the eggs she wouldn't have been up to working and would likely have spent more time in The Stove.'

'What be The Stove?'

'A shed half the size of your outhouse. It rested in the pasture by the Master's house and the sun beat upon it all day long. You be put inside and you cook.'

Clara's expression became one of disgust and she swallowed back against a touch of nausea. She glanced over her shoulder, gaze moving beyond the ladder. She raised herself on her haunches and could make out the top of the doors. They were closed on the darkening day, the sun to its bed and night rising from the east. There was no hint of her mother in the vicinity of the barn.

She reached forward and began to undo the rope about his ankles. Joshua withdrew his feet and she looked up at him.

'You shouldn't, Miss Clara,' he whispered in concern. 'Your Ma.'

'She'll not know 'til the morrow, by which time you'll have done proved that you've no intention of running away.' She shuffled forward and continued with the task.

'Will she not be angry?'

'It will not be a lasting anger, especially when you join us in the fields and swing the scythe. Without you much of the crop would be lost. With you there be hope to last the winter.

'The storm did more damage than stampeding cattle. The corn lies low and the mould sets in,' she explained, the rope coming free and Clara pulling it from him, seeing the soreness of his skin.

'Irritation only,' he stated, seeing the direction of her gaze and the guilt in her expression.

She looked to the bond about his wrists.

'Leave it be, Miss Clara,' he stated. 'I wouldn't have you add to your mother's wrath without cause. With legs free, I can be making my way to the fields. There be no needing to free my hands. I can still hold a scythe.'

'You sure?'

Joshua nodded.

A touch of light drew her gaze to a star peeking through a knot-hole in the slats over Joshua's shoulder. 'I should be returning,' she stated, her mother having warned her not to dawdle.

He held the bowl out to her. 'I must to my rest so as to gain more strength for the harvesting.'

'How goes your back?' she asked as she took the bowl and got to her feet.

'It mends.'

She peered over him and Joshua turned so Clara could see the healing wounds.

'Though the scars run deep and will be with me for the rest of my days.'

She frowned. 'I'm sorry.'

'You ain't got no reason to be sorrowful, Miss Clara,' stated Joshua as he turned back to her, his expression briefly tightening with pain. 'You didn't hold the whip or instruct its crack upon my skin.

'It were you and your Ma that saw me back from death's door, and for that I am forever in your debt. Helping with the harvest be but part payment and I would that there was more I could be doing.'

Her frown remained. 'We only done what any decent folk would have done.'

Joshua shook his head. 'You done more than anyone since my Ma and Pa.'

She glanced over her shoulder. 'I'd best be to the house.'

Joshua gave a nod as she turned and made her way to the ladder. He watched as she descended, making haste for fear of a scolding.

Rubbing the rawness about his ankles once she had exited the barn, he looked to the piece of rope lying on the floorboards and thought about taking flight. Though he could have probably undone the bond himself, he had not previously been in a fit state to do so, nor to entertain the possibility of running.

He looked to the rope about his wrists. He could most likely undo it by using his teeth and would have the night's length to make good his escape.

Using a beam for leverage, he got to his feet, keeping his head low. Testing his weight, he found his legs a little unwieldy after days without use. He bent and stretched them. The muscles ached, but there was strength enough to leave, to make passage through the darkness. He would have to take it slow and steady, but it could be done.

25

Clara entered the gloom of the cottage and discovered her mother seated in one of the lounging chairs to the left.

Lizbet wiped tears from her eyes as her daughter closed the door. 'I were just recalling me and your Pa sitting here on long winter nights,' she said softly, her voice filled with emotion.

Clara looked at the empty seat nearest the door, the dying light of day withdrawing through the open shutters opposite and highlighting the seat's emptiness in its slow departure. She placed the empty bowl on the corner of the table and then walked over.

Stopping before the chair, she stared at it thoughtfully. She imagined his hands resting upon the arms, the stains of their haunting presence darkening the wood, as if some small part of his existence had seeped into the grain and now existed as part of the timber.

'I'd sit on his knee as he done told me stories or talked of future dreams,' she commented.

Lizbet nodded, her eyes still glistening.

'The fire would be crackling in the hearth and you'd sew with the lantern resting on the dresser over your shoulder.'

'It'll be a long winter,' said her mother, looking out of the window, the trees beyond South Field filled with shadows and a solitary crow calling from within their concealment, its regular cry like a mocking laugh.

'Joshua be ready to help with the harvest. His strength is much returned,' stated Clara, feeling a swell of emotion and wishing to change the subject.

Lizbet continued to stare out of the window.

'Ma?'

She turned, blinking memories from her eyes.

'I say, Joshua be ready to help with the harvest,' she repeated. 'The poultice you done prepared has brung him back to health.'

Lizbet looked at her daughter, her eyes filled with the melancholia that arose from deep within. 'It may be we should tie him to one of the posts in the barn. That way there'll be no opportunity for him to flee.'

Clara felts her cheeks flush in the knowledge of removing the bonds about his ankles. 'I think he be staying put,' she said. 'He be safe here.'

'For the time being,' stated Lizbet pointedly.

She glanced back down at her father's chair. 'Can we be giving him one of Pa's shirts to wear in the field tomorrow?'

Her mother's eyes narrowed. 'Pardon?' There was an edge to her tone that set a warning in her daughter.

'I only ask 'cause you done burned his.'

'It were fit for nothing else,' replied Lizbet, 'and I ain't letting that nigger wear one of your Pa's shirts.'

Clara looked to the boards as she tried to think of something that may persuade her mother. 'It would be a kindness to me, not to him,' she said, raising her gaze once again. 'To conceal his diresome wounds from my eyes.'

'There ain't no way the nigger gonna be wearing one of your Pa's shirts,' she stated with conviction. 'You'll just be having to avert your gaze.'

'What if the sun subdues him with dizziness and fainting?'

'You be knowing little of the world, Clara,' she said with a frown and shake of her head. 'Niggers ain't like us. They be more like livestock. They can work in the heat without feeling it as we do.'

Clara looked out of the window to the field, the colour of the corn sapped by the fading light and the blight that had set in since the storm. 'It only be a small mercy,' she said quietly as she recalled bundling sheaves in the shadow of her father, trying to keep up with his pace in order to remain in the shade.

'Niggers be needing no mercy,' responded Lizbet.

She turned to her mother, still unused to the coldness with which she regarded Joshua's kind. It wasn't in keeping with the kindly woman she knew and there had been no hint as to its presence before. 'Even if he ain't in need of it, can't we be showing it to him.'

'Clara, he ain't having a shirt. Let that be the end of it.'

She looked at her mother for a little longer and then went over to the table, picking up the bowl and moving to the pail near the stove.

'If that be his then leave it by the chopping block. You can take it to The Eddy when morning comes.'

'He ain't contagious,' she said over her shoulder.

'What were that?'

Clara turned to her. 'I say, he ain't contagious.'

Lizbet regarded her sternly. 'You don't be knowing what he's got. Now, take the bowl out of the house or there'll be another switching.'

Clara glared back at her mother, feeling indignant and tempted to continue to the pail. The emotions that had arisen in response to her father's absence had been transformed by her mother's words in regards Joshua, anger rising in the stead of sadness.

Her courage not enough to continue towards the pail, she turned on her heels and made for the door. 'I don't be recognising you anymore,' she stated as she exited the cottage.

Lizbet got to her feet in a flurry of motion and stamped to the doorway. 'What did you say to me?'

Clara stood by the chopping block, holding the bowl in both hands as if seeking protection. 'Nothing,' she responded meekly.

'That weren't nothing that came out of your mouth as you stepped to the porch.'

'I were talking to Rosie,' she said, her eyes to the patchy grass.

'Funny, it sounded like you be addressing me,' replied Lizbet with an accusatory tone.

'Well, I weren't.' Clara briefly lifted her gaze to her mother's, but found the intensity of her eyes too much to bear.

Lizbet stared at her, knowing full well that the comment had been aimed at her. 'Put down the bowl and come inside. It be time for your bed.'

'It's but early.'

'And tiredness be making you ornery and agitated,' responded her mother. 'We'll begin with the harvest tomorrow and you'll be needing plenty of rest.'

Clara knew there was no point in argument. Her mother would not tolerate any further comments or protests, her tether at its end and the promise of a switching beckoning should she say a word out of line.

She put the bowl on the ground and stepped onto the porch, Lizbet moving aside and letting Clara enter before closing the door.

'Straight to bed with you,' said her mother, the words accompanied by an ushering motion.

She made her way down the hallway, passing into her room at the back of the cottage. The vague smell of potatoes greeted her as she shut the door and looked to the open shutters, the light all but vanquished by the depth of the darkness that followed on its shirttails, day and night chasing each other in endless repetition.

She took Rosie from the cord about her waist and looked at her shadowy face. 'I hope he don't run,' she stated quietly. 'Do you think I done the right thing?'

Rosie smiled in response.

'So do I,' she said with a nod, moving to the cot alongside the right-hand wall.

She rested the doll on the pillow and looked to the nightie which had been neatly laid out upon the cover. 'If we be wrong we'll find out in the morning,' she said as she began to undo the cord and ready herself for sleep.

26

Joshua ran through the darkness. Tree trunks surrounded him in every direction like the bars of an immense cage, the woodland backlit by a ghostly aura.

The hush was filled with the pounding of his heart and rush of blood as he pushed on. He sought liberty from the woods, feeling trapped and fearful.

The black shapes of men and dogs drew into the periphery of his vision and then fell back, haunting his every step. They were keeping pace but did not close in, savouring the hunt and content in watching his panicked flight.

Joshua realised in horror that there was no escape, that they had marshalled every step. His route was their making and his attempt to flee was futile.

He suddenly plunged into dark waters. The air was forced from his lungs by the icy grip, chest tightening with crushing force. Raising his hands with the last bubbles of expelled air, he found them tied as he sank into the thickness.

Joshua's feet touched the bottom and he found himself standing in a submerged forest. The boughs of the trees waved in the currents that stirred the water, the silver flecks of darting fish visible amongst them. The glow of torches shone from above and the muffled sound of men's voices mingled with the barking of dogs.

His eyes widened as he stared ahead, a huge and twisted tree materialising out of the gloom as he was carried forward by the flow. A figure hung from one of the branches, its back towards him. It slowly turned in an eddying current and Joshua saw his own face upon the man hanging lifeless in the noose.

He opened his mouth to let out a scream. The water rushed down his throat and searing pain erupted in his lungs.

Joshua woke with a start, eyes snapping open. He stared into the darkness, feeling the needling of straw against his back as the musty smells of the barn filled his nostrils.

Shivering as the perspiration on his face and torso cooled in the night air, he turned on his side to alleviate the irritation of his wounds. His heart was still pounding and he took deep breaths to calm the residue of terror clinging to him in the wake of the dream.

An owl hooted in the trees behind the barn as the images faded from his mind, all bar that of his face upon the hanged man. 'An omen?' he whispered into the stillness.

Joshua moved his hands beneath his head, able to make out the top of the ladder five yards from his position. He pondered the meaning of the dream, wondering if the macabre sight which had brought it to a shocking end related to running from the farmstead or remaining in place.

'Running,' he stated, what had preceded the image indicating that his end lay at the end of a rope if he chose to flee.

He took a deep breath, his pulse almost returned to normal. Thoughts of leaving continued to flit through his mind, but were pushed aside by the image of him hanging from the tree branch.

Joshua closed his eyes and tried to find sleep. His recovering stamina would be pushed to the limits when the new day came, but he'd worked under greater duress during his years on Benedict Farm. There had been times when he'd felt as though he would keel over in the fields, fall in the furrows to be planted like the cane, his spirit rising from the seed of his corpse.

'Here be different,' he stated to the night.

The girl had shown him kindness and consideration, was the first of the white folk to have done so. Though her mother looked upon him as most did, she had still made the poultice and helped him mend. There was no threat of the whip or a spell in The Stove.

'Here be different,' he repeated with a nod, the statement brought to an end with a yawn.

27

Clara approached the barn with a nervous stride, the birds waking to the dawn light. She hadn't slept well, tossing and turning as thoughts of Joshua running away persistently reoccurred. She'd been tempted to adjourn to the barn with the lantern to check on his continued presence, but the depth of the darkness had kept her beneath the cover of her cot.

As she looked to the slats, she prayed that he remained within, knowing that her mother's wrath would be severe if he had managed to flee thanks largely to her release of the bonds about his ankles. Though her faith in his word was strong, she could sympathise with his plight. She imagined the harsh existence he was running from and could comprehend the pressure it brought to bear when it came to wishing to escape such a life.

She reached for the left door and opened it apprehensively, stepping in and looking straight to the hayloft. She could see no evidence of Joshua and her pulse increased as she padded across the floor, hand moving to touch Rosie in comfort.

'Joshua?' she called from the foot of the ladder.

She heard movement above and he came into view, bent at the waist.

'Morning, Miss Clara,' he greeted. 'Should I come down?'

'There be time yet before we start the harvest. I came to...' She glanced around the barn's interior. '...Check on the rabbits,' she finished.

'I understand,' he responded knowingly. 'As you can plainly see, there ain't no cause to fret.'

Joshua stepped to the ladder and descended with care, the bond about his wrists meaning the activity was hampered. Setting foot on the compacted earth, he turned to her and then looked to the rabbit hutches.

She followed his gaze and then stepped over to the nearest. 'This be Elsa,' she stated, opening the door to the cage on the shelf.

Clara reached in and took out the large rabbit, who kicked and then settled against her chest. 'She be my favourite,' she added, stroking the creature's head as its nose twitched.

'She sure look soft.'

'Stroke her,' encouraged Clara, turning to him.

Joshua reached out and stroked Elsa's back with his bound hands. 'I only done felt one thing softer in all my life.'

'What were that?'

'My Ma's cheek,' he replied with a gentle smile as he stroked the rabbit some more, the creature's ears temporarily pressed down by the passage of his hands. 'I used to put mine to hers and close my eyes.'

'I hope you be seeing your parents again.'

The smile vanished and his attentions fell away from the rabbit in her arms. 'I ain't holding on to such hope,' he admitted.

Clara looked at his downcast expression and felt guilty at having raised the subject. She glanced at Elsa and placed her back into the hutch. 'I should be getting you some food to break the fast.'

Joshua nodded. 'Would be a fine thing before a day in the fields.'

She turned to leave and then paused. 'How do the heat affect you?' she enquired, recalling her mother's comments the previous evening.

'I don't like it much, but who do?' he replied. 'The beat of the sun can be making my mind swim and my body wearisome.'

She nodded, his words confirming her thoughts. 'I'll be sure to bring plenty of water and there'll be lunch when the sun be at its highest. You can find shade and rest awhile.'

'That be a welcome kindness,' he responded, knowing that his recuperation continued and it was likely his stamina would wane quicker than was usual as the day wore on.

Clara walked to the door and looked back over her shoulder as she passed out of the barn, Joshua watching and looking forlorn in the hollows of the building. She sighed as she set out towards the cottage, feeling the slight dampness of the earth against the soles of her feet. She thought about broaching the subject of giving Joshua one of Pa's shirts again, but dismissed it in light of the revelation she was going to have to make.

Stepping onto the porch, she went to the door and took a breath to bolster herself as she entered. Her mother was busying herself at the stove, her back to the entrance as she stirred the oatmeal in the cooking pot and steam rose to caress her cheeks.

'I heard you leave,' stated Lizbet without turning, wan light spilling in through the open shutters. 'Did you visit with the slave?'

'I went to see Joshua,' she replied, emphasising the last word. 'He be ready and willing to help with the harvest.' She left the door open and stepped to the table.

'Willing or not, he be lending his assistance.'

'I undid the rope about his ankles,' she blurted.

136

Lizbet turned sharply, wooden spoon stilled in her hand. 'Then you be going right back and retying it before he run.'

Clara shook her head. 'I untied it last evening and he still be here in the morning light.'

'Last evening!' Lizbet glared at her daughter. 'You didn't think to ask or tell?'

'I knew what you'd be thinking. You'd have sent me back to retie the rope.'

'What of his wrists?'

'They still be tied.'

Lizbet regarded her for a moment. 'I ain't happy one bit with what you've gone and done, Clara. What if he'd have run into the night? What if he'd been caught and revealed we offered him shelter here?'

Clara looked at her with a lack of comprehension.

'We be seen as nigger lovers. What's more, we be guilty of harbouring a fugitive.'

'A fugitive,' repeated Clara in disbelief.

Lizbet nodded, her gaze remaining fixed upon her daughter. 'Until he be returned to his Master, he be a fugitive,' she responded. 'He ain't no more than a runaway slave, Clara.

'Now, come and get some food,' she instructed, turning back to the cooking pot and removing it from the stove.

Clara paused and then made her way over, passing around the table. She moved to her mother's right and reached to the shelf over the basket of kindling to take down three bowls. Placing them on the cabinet by the stove, Lizbet glanced over.

'Be one of them for the negruh?'

She nodded her response.

'Then you can be putting it back and using the one out by the chopping block.'

Clara looked up at her. 'But that be used for stew last night and ain't been washed as yet,' she complained.

'He should be grateful to get any food at all,' responded her mother, taking the top bowl and reaching over her daughter to place it back on the shelf. 'Go fetch it and I'll dish out,' she stated, taking up the next bowl and holding it beside the cooking pot as she spooned out the oatmeal.

Clara walked back over to the door, passing onto the porch and down to where the bowl rested. Taking it up, she returned inside and put it beside the others, both filled with the pale and steaming food, one portion slightly smaller than the other.

Lizbet slopped a couple of spoonfuls into it and then made to pick up her bowl.

'That ain't enough,' said Clara. 'He gonna be working all day in the field and ain't long recovered.'

Lizbet frowned at her, but set her bowl back down and spooned more into Joshua's, scraping the last from the cooking pot. Clara looked at the dregs that rested on his serving, darkened by being burnt at the bottom of the pot.

'Have you anymore complaint to offer me on his behalf?' asked her mother with disapproval.

Clara slowly shook her head and picked up both her own and the slave's bowl before turning and stepping to the table.

'Let him wait,' stated Lizbet.

She set her bowl down and then hastened to the door with the other. 'It won't take but a minute,' she said over her shoulder as she exited with quick steps.

'Clara!' called Lizbet, her daughter already vanished from sight.

She made her way along the path, expectant of being called back from the porch, but the instruction to return not forthcoming. Entering the barn, she looked to the hutches, expecting to find Joshua still standing before them, but finding him absent.

'Joshua, I done brought you some food,' she called as she walked to the bottom of the ladder.

There was no response and no sound from above.

'Joshua?' Her brow creased and her pulse became elevated as silence once more greeted her enquiry.

Taking hold of the right side of the ladder and holding the steaming bowl firmly in her other hand, the tip of her thumb against the warmth of its contents, she made her way up. Reaching the top rungs, she peered into the hayloft and found it empty.

Narrowing her eyes, Clara stared into the corner where Joshua usually abided, as if trying to will him into sight. The shadows beneath the eaves remained vacant and her heart raced.

'Has he done taken flight?' she asked, Rosie hanging mute at her waist. 'Maybe he be hearing what Ma say and her words have set him to running,' she said worriedly.

The creak of the doors drew her gaze over her shoulder and she found Joshua entering the barn. He looked up at her and noted the expression of concern upon her face.

'I be visiting the outhouse,' he stated, scratching his beard.

Clara took a breath and made her way back down the ladder as he walked over to her. 'For you,' she stated, holding out the bowl.

'Much obliged, Miss Clara,' he replied, taking it from her with a nod of thanks.

'I forgot to be bringing a spoon.'

'Won't be the first time I be using my fingers,' he said with a disarming smile, 'but it'll be the first time I've something hot to eat in the morning.'

'It'll give you the strength to see through the say,' she stated. 'I must return before Ma comes a hunting for me.'

Joshua nodded and she stepped past him, making for the door and passing outside. He watched her leave and then moved to the sacks of vegetables against the wall. Seating himself, he used two fingers to scoop out the oatmeal, sniffing its fading heat before placing it in his mouth and chewing in silence as the day brightened.

28

Joshua swung the scythe, his back bent as he held the implement halfway along its length, his hands still bound and the unusual grip initially proving cumbersome. The blade cut through a swathe of corn, the already low stems dropping further against those beyond. He wiped sweat from his brow and glanced up at the blazing sun before looking over his shoulder, barely a quarter of South Field as yet harvested.

Lizbet was gathering sheaves in his wake, her face flushed by the effort as she stood them together, looking at the mildew that had taken to some of the grains with dissatisfaction. Clara watched from the porch, seated on the edge with Rosie held upon her lap as the morning wore on.

The scythe arced once again, his muscles straining and shoulders beginning to burn in the brightness. He could already feel his strength being sapped by labouring in the heat, his recovery not as close to full health as he'd thought.

Taking a step forward and swinging again, he worried that he would not last out the day. 'I be pushing through before,' he mumbled to himself, determined to do his best.

'What were that?' asked Lizbet.

'Nothing, Mistress,' he replied over his shoulder, using the only form of address he had ever used in regards white women.

'Be sure to cut the corn low,' she commented.

'It be easier if my hands were free to take a proper hold.'

'You be working fine as you are,' she replied without sympathy.

Joshua resumed the cutting, blinking perspiration from his eyes. Clara set Rosie on the step of the porch and took up one of the cups nearby. Dipping it into the pail at her feet, she rose and made her way out into the field, the stubble scraping her shins.

'That be well timed,' stated her mother as she straightened and looked to her daughter, gaze falling on the cup.

'It be for Joshua,' she responded without censoring her words.

Lizbet's expression clouded. 'The negruh before your Ma?'

Clara halted and proffered the cup, head bowed.

Lizbet looked upon her daughter a moment and then took the refreshment. She raised it to her mouth and drank it down without pause, wiping her lips as she swallowed the last.

'Now you can be seeing to the negruh,' she stated, holding the vessel back out to her daughter.

Clara took it and turned without raising her head. She went back to the pail and took another cup from the porch boards, giving Rosie a look which expressed her annoyance and frustration. Filling it, she moved back into the field and went to Joshua.

The scythe lifted and swung before coming to rest. He leant on its long handle and took the cup with a nod. 'Much obliged,' he stated before taking a drink.

'Don't dawdle,' stated Lizbet as she stood two sheaves together and set about bundling another.

Joshua glanced at her and then downed the rest of the water. Passing the cup back to Clara, he took up the scythe and set to harvesting once again.

'Ain't it soon time for lunch?' asked Clara, looking to her mother.

'When half be done, then we break for food.'

Clara looked about the field, seeing there was a good deal to be cut before the halfway point was reached. 'But it be nearly midday already.'

'I ain't in control of the time,' said Lizbet, her words snappy as the heat and the scratch of stalks prickled her mood. 'If the negruh be working with greater pace we'd be about there by now.'

Clara's brow tightened. She'd witnessed the trouble Joshua had encountered due to the bonds about his wrists and thought her mother's comment unfair. 'If you'd have untied his hands, you mean.'

Lizbet went still, stooped as she gathered up stalks of corn. She turned to her daughter with a hard stare. 'Go inside,' she instructed with a low tone that carried the threat of punishment should another word be spoken.

Clara managed to hold her gaze a moment and then set off towards the cottage, collecting Rosie from the porch as she passed within. She moved to the window near the table and looked out to the field with fierce eyes, her gaze lingering on her mother's bent form.

'We knows the truth of it,' she stated, raising Rosie and looking to the doll's face as she stroked her hair briefly, the action calming her.

Placing Rosie on the table, she took up the broom from beside the door. She moved to the rear of the main room and began to sweep the dust towards the entrance, the activity helping to lift her tension further.

'Yes, we sure knows the truth of it,' she reiterated as the switches scraped over the boards and motes of golden dust swirled in the sunlight that slanted in through the doorway.

29

The sun hung low in the west, peering over the treetops on the far side of The Eddy. Joshua swung the scythe, cutting the last of the corn in South Field and staggering under the momentum of the tool.

Clara looked over as she gathered stalks, her mother having adjourned to the house in order to prepare supper. She watched as he righted himself, her expression filled with concern. It was clear from the way he leant on the implement that he was close to exhaustion.

'You can be resting now,' she stated, 'I can gather the last of it without need of help.'

Joshua regarded her and then glanced at the cottage. Though he could not see her, he was sure that Lizbet kept a close eye on their progress from within the gloom. 'I will help,' he said simply, bending with a wince of pain and laying the scythe on the stubble.

He stepped over to her and they gathered sheaves side by side, crouched and tying the bundles before standing them together. The last stalks were collected and it wasn't long until Clara stood the final sheaf. She straightened and put her hands to her lower back, her face glistening and arms irritated by the scratch of the corn.

'Done,' she said, smiling thinly at him and unable to fathom how he had worked the entire day. She had laboured for only a few hours and every second was felt in the ache of her muscles.

'Supper be ready,' called Lizbet from the doorway, both of them looking over as she wiped her hands with a cloth.

Joshua nodded to himself, her appearance having the timing of someone who'd been watching and confirming his suspicion that she'd been doing so.

'Come,' said Clara with a nod towards the cottage before setting off.

He began after her, his steps heavy with the weight of weariness.

'The scythe,' shouted Lizbet, pointing.

Joshua stopped and glanced back at the implement.

'I'll get it,' said Clara, turning.

'Let the negruh fetch it. It were him that left it there.'

Clara glanced at her mother unhappily as Joshua made for the scythe, bending and retrieving it with a tight expression. She looked at the deep scars crosshatching his back and had to avert her gaze, unable to face the foulness of what had been wrought upon him for the kindly use of two eggs.

Waiting for him to reach her, Clara then fell in step beside Joshua, neither of them finding words as they made their way across the field to the cottage. She climbed the step first and walked in, Lizbet turning from the stove as she dished up the mutton stew.

'The nigger eats on the porch,' she stated as Joshua was about to enter.

'What?' Clara looked at her in astonishment.

'He ain't coming in and he certainly ain't taking your Pa's place at the table.'

'But he just be spending the day harvesting South Field for us.'

'That's as may be, but he can still eat on the porch.' She held a bowl towards her daughter after putting a couple of thick slices of bread into it. 'Give it him and then take your seat.'

Clara opened her mouth to protest further.

'It be fine, Miss Clara,' said Joshua behind her. 'I be grateful for the food,' he added, smiling thinly at Lizbet.

Clara glanced over her shoulder and then went around the table to get the bowl, taking it back to him. He nodded his thanks as he took it and turned, stepping down onto the dry earth and seating himself on the porch.

She looked at the lashes upon his back once again. The low angle of the sun highlighted the ridges and the thought that he was still being treated with unfairness served to fuel a sense of righteous indignation. She went to the nearest chair and pulled it out with force before sitting heavily.

'Looks like it be another early night for you,' commented her mother as she placed a bowl before her.

'Looks like it be more unkindness for Joshua,' she responded heatedly under her breath.

'I'll not have any sharp tongue from you, young girl, unless you fancy skipping supper and going straight to your bed.'

Clara glanced up at her hotly, but said nothing more as her mother took the seat opposite and looked at her pointedly, placing her hands together in readiness for prayer.

With a sigh, Clara followed suit and bowed her head.

'For what we are about to receive, may the Good Lord make us thankful,' said Lizbet.

'Amen,' they finished together.

Clara reached for one of the slices of bread resting beside her bowl and violently tore off a piece, using it to collect up some of the stew before pushing it into her mouth. Wiping a drip from her chin, she chewed with agitation as Lizbet took up a spoon and began to tuck into her food, the cottage filled with a pressing hush as they consumed the meal.

'If you don't be slowing yourself, you'll get dyspepsia,' scolded Lizbet.

Clara made no acknowledgement of her mother's words and didn't slow the pace of her consumption.

'Clara!' she snapped.

Her daughter's gaze lifted and was filled with scorn. 'I heard you.'

'And yet you still eat like a pig to the trough.'

'I eat how I want to eat,' replied Clara rebelliously.

'I'll be to the crick to wash myself,' said Joshua through the open door. 'You want I should wash the bowl?' he asked, holding the vessel at an angle so they couldn't see he had yet to finish his meal, but was merely providing a timely interruption before things got too heated between mother and daughter.

They both turned to him as he peered into the growing darkness, the sun now hidden beyond the trees in the west. Lizbet simply nodded her response, the rising tide of her anger abating.

'I could take yours when you be done.'

'Clara will take them when you return,' she replied, meeting her daughter's glance when she looked over at her.

Joshua gave a nod and stepped from the porch. He walked ponderously to the gate in the low fence and passed through, moving along the short path to the mudflats where the stream turned westward and hoping that his intervention had served to diffuse the situation in the house.

He crouched and in order to finish his food, the trees at the bend creaking and the sound of crickets arising from the undergrowth that edged the flats. He wiped the final sliver of bread around the inside of the bowl and licked the last from his fingers before placing the vessel upon the cracked mud.

Standing, he took off his britches and carefully slipped into the water. The surface rippled about his midriff as a dragonfly skimmed by, the sound of its rapid flight drawing his gaze. It passed through a beam of sunlight that made passage through the trees on the far side, its fragile wings glittering and golden.

Joshua watched it awhile, allowing the weight of the day to lift from him, the waters drawing out the heat and stiffness held within his body. He splashed his shoulders, rubbed the tops of his arms and the back of his neck, closing his eyes as he did so.

Birds called in the strand of woodland that largely hid the dipping sun and he smiled to himself. He didn't know their names, but knew his lack of knowledge didn't make their appearance or their songs any less beautiful.

He began to idly hum a tune as he bathed, realising after a short while that it was Clara's song for her doll. His smile broadened and he turned towards the flats in readiness to pull himself out.

'Howdy,' greeted Clara as she crouched at the waterside with bowls and cups piled in her hands. There was a grin on her face, though a touch of tension remained in her expression after the altercation with her mother. 'That be my song for Rosie.'

Joshua nodded. 'It came to mind without bidding,' he responded.

'Can you swim?'

He shook his head. 'It be lucky that wading be all that's needed,' he joked.

Clara chuckled, the last of her tension dissipating.

'Can you?' he asked.

'Nope, and it be too deep for me to wade.'

'That be a shame. It be a welcome refreshment.'

149

She shrugged and her smile faded.

He noted the change and dipped his hands into the water, splashing her with sprays of droplets.

She raised an arm before her face and fell back onto the dry mud, chuckling as a few drops glistened upon her face and the topmost cup tumbled to the ground and rolled towards the water.

Joshua reached out and picked it up. 'I be thinking you could do with a wash,' he grinned, righting the cup on the baked mud.

She laughed again and wiped a droplet from her nose. 'Ma'll be down shortly and we'll both be washing the day from our skin,' she stated, her eyes much brightened by the light-hearted interaction.

Joshua moved to her right and hauled himself from the water. 'Could you be passing my bowl?'

'I can wash it for you,' replied Clara.

He shook his head. 'It'll give me time to dry,' he said, holding out his hand as he crouched on the bank.

She put down the pile of items she was carrying and passed him the bowl. He leant forward, holding it in the water and rubbing the interior with his free hand.

Clara watched and then took up the cup which had fallen from the pile. She pushed herself up onto her haunches and shuffled to the creek's edge, dipping it in and beginning to clean it with her fingers.

Finishing his task, Joshua rose and stepped behind her. Placing the bowl on the ground, he took up his britches and put them on. 'I'd best be to the barn,' he stated as he stooped to pick up the bowl once again, his expression tightening with the aches and pains that resided within his tired body.

'I'll take that back,' she said, glancing at it.

He nodded and passed it to her wet hands. 'Till the morning,' he stated, turning and making for the gate as day turned to dusk and the western horizon began to turn a burnt orange.

30

Joshua wearily made his way up the ladder, his body aching to the bone. Reaching the top, he heard scurrying and saw the dark shape of a rat run into the shadows at the rear, the sound of claws upon wood marking the beast's descent from the hayloft.

He made his way over to the thin bed of straw, almost falling upon it as he reached the corner. Settling upon his side, he looked out at the web-shrouded eaves of the barn. His gaze was attracted by movement and he watched as a beetle passed across the boards before his face, its black carapace with a green sheen in the last light of day.

Closing his eyes, he expected sleep to come quickly, but the image of him hanging from the submerged tree drew up from the depths of his mind. He tried to push it aside, but it persisted.

Joshua raised his lids and stared ahead. He turned on his back with a grimace and looked at the underside of the shingles, noting a hole through which the deep blue of the sky could be seen. His thoughts were purposefully turned to the brief but happy exchange with Clara at the creek, hoping that the fresh memory would dispel the remnant of the previous night's dream.

His strategy was successful for a while, a thin smile gracing his lips as he remembered the girl's laughter. The tiredness which lay upon him drew his thoughts away from the images, his ability to concentrate reduced.

The hanging figure drew back into his mind.

Joshua pushed himself into a sitting position, feeling the pressure of his bladder. With a sigh, he gathered the strength to rise and went back to the ladder.

Passing down, his foot slipped and he nearly lost his grip on the sides, for a brief moment thinking he was going to fall to the floor. His pulse elevated, he clung motionless for a while, face to one of the rungs as he regained his composure.

Making his way to the ground with the slight tremble of adrenalin in his weakened legs, he walked unsteadily to the doors. He exited the barn and went round to the eastern side, furthest from the cottage. Leaning a shoulder against the wall slats, he relieved himself and felt the cool touch of the night gathering in the air, steam rising from his outpouring.

Joshua shambled back into the barn and stopped just inside the doors, his gaze to the thick shadows of the hayloft. He had no urge to rejoin them and didn't relish the thought of climbing the ladder once again.

He glanced around, hoping to find some distraction from the image that haunted him. His gaze fell on Elsa's hutch and he walked towards it with a nod.

Turning the fastening and opening the door, he reached in and carefully withdrew the rabbit. She kicked out with her back legs, but soon settled against him, her softness to his bare chest. He turned and made his way over to the sacks by the opposite wall, seating himself and leaning against them.

The smell of earth and vegetables filled his nose as he cradled Elsa and stroked her with lulling regularity. He closed his eyes, stretching out his legs and letting his cradling arm rest upon his lap. Yawning, he savoured the touch of the rabbit's fur and his hazy thoughts turned to his mother. Her face was vague after the years that had passed since he'd last seen her, but her kindly eyes remained in sharp focus, the soft creases at their edges adding to the impression of warmth.

A tear snaked down his cheek as the attention he paid to Elsa slowed. His hand finally fell still, head tipping to the side as sleep overcame him, his mother's image managing to withstand the persistence of the hanging tree.

31

'Time to rise.'

Clara opened her sore eyes and looked at her mother as she stood in the doorway to her room. 'It be morning already?' she groaned, stretching as she yawned.

'The sun be almost up,' responded Lizbet as her daughter wiped a tired tear from her cheek with the back of her hand. 'When you've done had your breakfast, I want you to be opening the coop and then there be washing to be done at The Eddy.'

'I need to feed the rabbits and their bedding may be in need of changing,' said Clara as she sat up on her cot and rubbed her eyes.

'You've the whole day, just make sure all your chores get done.' Lizbet turned and went to the main room as Clara swung her legs over the side of the bed.

She rolled her head around on her shoulders, feeling the ache brought on by the gathering she'd done the previous evening. 'If I ache from only a little work, then Joshua must be as stiff as a board,' she commented, glancing at Rosie as she rested by the pillow.

She stood and rubbed the back of her neck as she stepped to the window. Opening the shutters, she spied a thin plume of white smoke rising to the north-east. Her brow became furrowed and her eyes narrowed as she stared through the trees, realising that the fumes arose from a different location to that which she'd seen before.

Pondering their cause, she turned and took off her nightie, laying it over the foot of the bed. Crouching and dragging a wooden box from beneath, she selected a faded yellow dress. She dropped it over her head and tied the waist with the piece of cord lying on the shelves by the door before tucking Rosie at her waist and exiting the room.

She could smell the oatmeal in the hallway and her mouth watered in response. Her stomach moaned as she entered the main room and went to the table, yawning again as she took the nearest seat.

Lizbet stepped over with a bowl in each hand, placing one before her daughter before sitting to her left.

'For what we are about to receive, let the Good Lord make us thankful.'

'Amen,' they finished together.

Lizbet picked up the spoon already resting at her place and looked over, noting Clara glance towards the cabinet in expectancy of seeing another bowl resting there. 'Don't fret, there be another portion in the pot.'

Clara began to rise.

'The negruh can wait,' stated her mother.

Clara saw the hardness in her gaze and settled back on the chair. 'He done worked all yesterday and will be needing it more than me,' she complained.

'He'll have to wait.' There was no concession in her tone.

Clara sagged and reached for her spoon. She blew on the oatmeal before taking up the first mouthful, wanting to consume it quickly so as to visit with Joshua at the barn.

Lizbet frowned at her daughter, seeing her eagerness. 'You'll go and burn your tongue,' she warned, 'but maybe that ain't such a bad thing considering its sharpness of late.'

Clara glanced over surreptitiously, keeping her head low, her gaze unkind. She barely paused as she devoured the basic meal, feeling the heat of the oats and her cheeks flushing despite her wish not to show any outward sign to her mother. She placed the spoon in her bowl when she was done and pushed her seat back.

'Can't you be waiting 'til I'm done?'

'I'll come back to collect the bowls when Joshua has been fed,' she replied, sidestepping the question as she passed behind her mother and went to the stove.

Lizbet shook her head and looked out of the window opposite her, a sense of satisfaction stirring as her gaze settled on the stubble and sheaves that were evidence of the previous day's labour. 'We'd better gather them into the barn once the sun has done dried them,' she muttered to herself as Clara took a clean bowl from the shelf above the kindling.

'I beg your pardon?' she asked her mother.

'Oh, nothing,' responded Lizbet, turning her attention back to her food.

Clara took up the large wooden spoon resting in the cooking pot and then lifted the pot itself. Her arm strained as she tried to tip its weight, its lower end resting on the hob. She spooned the oatmeal from within and then scraped the residue from the edges and bottom, chasing it up the side and letting it drip thickly into the bowl.

Happy to see that it still steamed with warmth, she let the pot rest back in place and opened the cabinet in order to retrieve a spoon.

'He can be using his fingers,' said Lizbet without needing to turn, fully aware of what her daughter was doing.

Clara looked at the back of her mother's head, a flare of anger burning in her eyes. 'Why do you hate him so?'

Lizbet looked down at the remainder of her breakfast. 'I don't hate the negruh...'

'Joshua,' Clara put in.

'I don't hate him, I just be knowing his kind. You ain't seen no niggers before, Clara. They be dirty and simple, only suited to labour and service.' She turned to look at her daughter. 'They ain't like us white folk.'

'He don't seem no different.'

'Would you have done stayed in the barn knowing your life were in danger? You undid the bonds about his legs and yet he didn't run,' she said. 'He didn't run 'cause he be simpleminded and born to serve.'

Clara pondered. 'But he done run from his Master.'

'Only because he were put to the whip,' responded Lizbet, 'but that'll have only earned him a noose and a sharp drop.'

Clara expression fell and Lizbet realised what she'd said. She'd tried to avoid the raw truth, but thought that maybe it was time her daughter faced it.

'They'll hang him?'

Lizbet nodded solemnly. 'Most likely.'

'Then we must keep him here,' pleaded Clara, 'and you can't be going to Tyler.'

'If we're discovered to be harbouring him then jail be my destination, at best.'

'At best,' Clara held her mother's gaze.

'At worst, we find ourselves dangling beside him.'

Clara blanched and felt faint, her hand going to the stove for support. Lizbet readied herself to go to her daughter's aid should she fall.

'It be time for you to know the truth,' she stated regretfully. 'The world ain't a kindly place of dolls and games. It be harsh and fearsome. To survive you must develop the skin of a horned toad, thick and tough.

'You've been living a sheltered life. That be mine and your Pa's fault to a stretch, but now things need to change.'

'I don't want things to be a changing.'

'There ain't no want or don't want in this, Clara. They gonna change and there ain't nothing you can do about it.'

'They really be hanging us?' asked her daughter softly.

'You be too young to recall old Thaddeus Carter. He be accused of sympathising with niggers and was found at the bottom of his pond with a millstone about his neck soon thereafter. They say men came in the night and carried out Biblical justice. Over in Clay County they hung a husband and wife for harbouring a nigger only last year.'

'They gonna come in the night for us?'

Lizbet shook her head. 'Ain't nobody but us knows the negruh be here. I need to tell Tyler before anyone discovers the truth so we don't suffer for his sake.'

'But no one comes by the farm,' said Clara, looking to the trees beyond the harvested corn, a sense of foreboding arising within as she imagined eyes watching from the shadows, the sense of security that hung over the farmstead tainted by her mother's revelations.

'They be looking for him, you mark my words.'

She turned her gaze back to her mother. 'We can hide him.'

'Clara, there ain't no way around this.'

'If there was, would you take it?'

Lizbet took a breath. 'There ain't.'

Clara looked to the bowl of oatmeal, its steam barely visible as it cooled on the cabinet. 'When will you go?'

'A day, maybe two. When the harvest is good and done.'

'So you'll be taking advantage and then leaving Joshua to his fate once he's done saved us from a lean winter?' There was disgust in her tone.

'What would you have me do?' asked Lizbet with growing heat in her tone. 'Would you have us starve or die at the negruh's side?'

'I've done told you before, he be called Joshua,' said Clara angrily, taking up the bowl from the cabinet and making for the door.

Lizbet pushed her chair back, spoon still in hand. The sound of its legs scraping on the floor filled the cottage as she barred her daughter's way. 'His name ain't important,' she said forcefully. 'He be passing through on his way to the next life, and unless you want to be joining him real soon, you'll mind your tongue and accept what has to be done.'

Clara stared down at the floorboards.

'Do you understand?'

There was no response.

'Answer me, darn it!' snapped Lizbet.

Clara flinched. 'I understand,' she said after a hesitation, refusing to meet her mother's gaze.

Lizbet studied her a while and then pulled her chair in to allow her daughter to pass. Clara moved behind her and went to the door, exiting the house with head bowed.

She walked along the path, glancing nervously at the trees at the bottom of South Field. She could feel eyes peering from the last remnants of the night, the shadows lingering in the undergrowth beneath the boughs.

Clara walked into the barn with the bowl cupped in her hands. Her gaze was immediately drawn to the open door of Elsa's hutch and her eyes widened.

Looking around the interior, she saw Joshua lying on the dusty floor in front of the sacks. To her relief, the rabbit was sitting between him and Bella's empty stall, eating a beet that she had pulled from a hole in the sackcloth.

'Joshua?' she said as she walked over to him.

There was no response and she was struck by the fearful thought that he had been overcome by the efforts of the previous day combined with his weakened condition. She looked for the tell-tale rise and fall of his chest, feeling relief when she spied shallow breathing.

Clara crouched before him and reached out to touch his shoulder. 'Joshua,' she stated with greater volume.

His eyes slowly opened and he blinked away initial blurriness.

'It be time to break the fast.'

Joshua's gaze moved past her to the slats of the far wall, seeing golden light through cracks and holes. 'The sun's already risen,' he observed in surprise, unable to recall any previous occasion when he had been allowed or able to sleep so long.

'You must have be needing such rest,' responded Clara, holding the bowl out to him. 'Here. Eat.'

He raised himself into a sitting position, his body filled with aches. Taking the bowl with a nod of gratitude, he put his fingers into the lukewarm offering and began to consume breakfast.

Clara settled back and watched, her mother's words about hangings and millstones echoing down the corridors of her mind and a feeling of deep compassion arising in response. She looked upon Joshua with an ache in her heart, wishing there were some action she could undertake to ensure his safety, but unable to arrive at any solution.

He glanced up at her and paused in his eating as he regarded her curiously. 'Be there something amiss?' he asked after swallowing, his pulse increasing as he considered the possibility that her mother had decided to inform the authorities of his presence.

She shook her head, but found no words with which to reply, her throat constricted as a tide of emotion arose from her depths.

Joshua's ominous sense of his time at the farm reaching its conclusion grew stronger in sight of her reaction. He felt sickened and saw tears glistening in the girl's eyes. 'Be you sure?'

Clara nodded. 'Me and Ma be out of sorts,' she said in an attempt to explain her condition, wiping her eyes with the back of her hand. 'Hot words were spoken.'

He studied her expression for a moment. 'I hope they not be on my account.'

She shook her head once more, but was unable to meet his gaze.

'I'll not be staying. You knows that,' he stated, guessing at the truth. 'You'll be here with your Ma when I've done gone, so it best you keep good terms.'

'But she don't see you,' she responded, raising her eyes to his. 'She sees what the world has told her to see.'

'I knows it and you knows it. That be good enough.'

'It ain't good enough,' she complained.

'It has to be,' he said. 'You see the truth of it and in that there be hope for the future.'

Joshua glanced down at the oatmeal and then turned to look at Elsa when he noted movement to his right. 'I'm sure glad she ain't run off. I took her out when sleep didn't come.'

Clara looked to the rabbit, who was finishing the last of the beet. She did not respond, her thoughts still lingering on what had been said.

'Best you back to the cottage. I'll be finishing and ready for work soon enough.' He dipped his fingers into the cold oats, a residue of faint heat at their centre.

Clara stayed before him awhile and then stood. She went to Elsa and took the creature into her arms. Stoking the rabbit's silken fur, she conveyed her back to the hutch, giving her a kiss on the head before placing her inside.

Fastening the door, she glanced over her shoulder, finding Joshua scraping the last from the bowl as he sat before the sacks. The early sunlight penetrated the east-facing wall behind the hutches and cast him in a warm haze. The image was dreamlike and captivating, Clara committing it to memory.

Detecting her stillness, he glanced up and their gazes met. He saw the contemplative look upon her youthful face and wondered at its origin.

Without a word, Clara went to the doors and passed out of the barn. Joshua stared after her as the light streaming through gaps in the far wall became more defined, the sun's strength growing as it climbed higher into the sky.

32

Clara knelt at the edge of The Eddy, the mud beneath her knees pliable and darkened by penetrating water. She rubbed the shirt her mother had worn the previous day against the washboard leant against her knees, rocking back and forth as she hummed her song for Rosie. Her mood had brightened considerably with the rising of the sun and thanks to the time that had drawn out since the earlier altercation.

Holding the shirt up before her, she paid special attention to the cuffs and collar. Finding them clean to her satisfaction, she wrung it out with a practised twist. Folding it, she placed the shirt into the basket set to her left.

Looking to the items remaining upon her lap, she took up a pair of her father's britches which her mother had been using. She idly ran her fingers along the bottom of the legs, the material frayed with wear.

Beginning the tune once again in order to push back the thought that her father would never return, she leant forward and placed the britches into the water, making sure to soak them through before lifting and lightly wringing them. They were taken to the board and she set to cleaning them, changing her grip from time to time so that the whole garment felt the rub.

She dipped them back into the water and ignored the rawness of her palms caused by the roughness of the cord. Her thoughts turned to her mother and Joshua working in the east fields and she hoped they fared well. She had not seen them since their departure, but had been busy with her chores.

Clara glanced up, seeing that the sun would not be long in reaching its zenith. When it did, she would pass into the east fields with a pail of water and check on the progress of the harvest.

Holding up the britches, she nodded to herself and wrung them out. They were placed in the basket and she settled back a moment, staring upstream. Her mother's words concerning the punishment brought to bear upon those aiding and abetting negroes came to mind and she frowned. A distinct feeling of unease came over her, as it had when the words had first been spoken.

The creak of the trees on the far side of The Eddy drew her gaze, a look of mild fear upon her face. She peered at the undergrowth, the hairs on her arms tingling as she sought any sign that she were being watched.

Movement caught her eye and Clara turned sharply to the right. A large snake was making its way out of the brush onto the sun-baked mud, its scales burnt gold and patterned with dark brown.

She let out a yell of fright and leapt up, the washboard tumbling forward and splashing into the creek. The rattlesnake drew its head back defensively as her heel sank into the edge of the bank and she fought to retain her balance, arms out to the sides.

The earth gave way beneath her weight and Clara fell back. She released a scream as she toppled into the waters, seeing glittering droplets rising into the clear sky before her sight was obscured by the wash of entry and she was forced to close her eyes.

She struggled and kicked, arms flailing wildly. She managed to raise her face above the surface and let out another scream, water spilling into her mouth. She spluttered and spat, fighting for breath.

'JOSHUA!' she yelled before the water drew her back into its depths.

33

Joshua swung the scythe and a swathe of corn fell. His progress was slower than the previous day, his body not yet returned to full health and strength waning. The heat was building and he paused to wipe a bead of sweat from his eyes, glancing back at Lizbet. She was busied in the task of gathering, bent and brooding. They had said no more than a few words upon first setting out to the east fields, but since arrival only silence had filled the gulf between them.

He lifted the scythe and swung again, sure the woman's dour mood was related to the heated words that Clara had mentioned. He thought about enquiring, but held his tongue, knowing that white folk didn't care to share their business with his kind, nor did they welcome the intrusion.

His brow furrowed as he raised the tool into the air, his grip still hampered by the bonds about his wrists. There had been a shrill call at the edge of his hearing, one that prickled the nape of his neck.

'You be hearing that?' he asked, lowering the scythe.

Lizbet straightened and looked over at him, her expression stern. 'I hear nothing but the absence of reaping,' she replied pointedly.

Joshua frowned, wondering at the sound he felt sure had arisen to the west and looking to the trees that veiled the buildings and South Field. Shaking his head, he lifted the implement once again.

A scream arose as the blade swept down, its origin unmistakable.

Joshua dropped the scythe without hesitation. Setting off, he sprinted across the harvested portion of the field, ignoring the sting of the stubble against his soles as he wove between the sheaves.

'Where be you...?'

'JOSHUA!' The cry was filled with desperate urgency.

Lizbet turned to the trees with a look of horror. 'Clara!' she exclaimed, setting off after the slave, who was already obscured from view as he took the path back to the house and passed through the strand of woodland.

Joshua's pulse raced and adrenalin added to the urgent pumping of his blood as he ran along the track, passing the barn. He looked for some sign of Clara's whereabouts, eyes wide as he neared the cottage, his pace unrelenting.

He heard the disturbance of water and immediately set his gaze beyond the boundary fence. Running alongside the porch and past the chopping block, he leapt the fence without pause, seeing motion in The Eddy as he vaulted.

Making haste to the mudflats, he briefly scanned the surface before leaping in. His feet touched the bottom and he ducked his head under, forcing his eyes to remain open and searching. He saw her sunken in the murky waters, dark hair drifting about her head and arms limp as her body floated just above the mud.

Breaking the surface with a gasp, Joshua wiped water from his eyes as he waded to her position. He ducked back under and gathered Clara into his arms, pushing upward and resurfacing in a shower of glittering droplets.

He blinked his vision clear and looked down at her face. Her eyes were closed and her expression taut with pain. He moved his gaze to her chest, praying to see even the slightest sign of movement, but finding none.

Lizbet hurried onto the mudflats, her face wrought with distress. 'NO!' she cried, holding her arms out towards them as she came to a halt on the bank. 'Lord, don't take her from me,' she pleaded, glancing heavenward.

Joshua waded towards her and she took her daughter from his arms, drops of water falling from her stillness. She fell to her knees and cradled Clara against her chest, holding her with the tightness of love's yearning.

'Come back,' she said, voice thick with emotion.

Joshua climbed out of the creek and looked down upon them, his body trembling after his efforts. He wiped his eyes once again, feeling helpless in sight of the sad embrace.

Clara's body suddenly convulsed and coughing burst from her small form. Water spilled out of the sides of her mouth and sprayed into the air as she expelled what had found its way into her lungs.

'Clara!' exclaimed Lizbet, wiping her daughter's brow and filled with such relief that she was overcome by momentary dizziness.

Joshua quickly crouched, supporting her shoulder with a gentle hand. She glanced back at him. Her eyes were filled with tears and she held his gaze a moment as if looking into his soul.

'I'm sorry, Ma.'

The rasping words drew their attention back to the bedraggled form resting in Lizbet's arms.

'There ain't no need to be sorry,' said Lizbet, stroking her daughter's wet hair.

'There were a snake,' she croaked, 'come to sun itself on the flats.' She coughed and struggled for breath as Joshua scanned the mud, finding no trace of the reptile.

'Save your words, there'll be time enough for them later. You're safe, and that be all that matters now,' said Lizbet.

'We need to be getting you into some dry clothes,' she added, standing and bearing the full weight of her daughter.

'I can walk,' stated Clara.

'You sure?'

She nodded and Lizbet carefully set her down upon her feet, keeping hold of her upper arm in case Clara's assessment of her own condition proved inaccurate. She stood unsteadily and spat creek water from her mouth, her lungs still giving her pain with each breath.

Lizbet turned to Joshua and gave a nod towards the few pieces of washing lying on the mud. He responded in kind to indicate he understood her meaning and began to gather up the items that had been thrown from Clara's lap when first she'd spied the snake.

Helping her daughter, Lizbet and Clara made their way from the flats and along the path to the gate. They passed through as Joshua picked up the basket of clean washing, the dirty hung over his arm. He scanned the undergrowth beside the bank for any sign of the rattlesnake and his gaze settled on Rosie as she rested in the water by a bed of reeds.

Cradling the basket in the crook of his arm, he stepped over and retrieved the doll, which was saturated and equal in bedragglement to the girl. Squeezing her, he watched the water run over his fingers and drip to the mud and then laid Rosie on top of the clean washing.

Turning, he made his way to the cottage and set the basket on the porch. 'I'll be to the harvest,' he called, not wishing to enter without permission and hearing mother and daughter in a room to the rear.

There was no response and he walked away, soaked britches clinging to his legs and the water serving to cool him beneath the beat of the sun. He made his way back to the east fields, passing into the one on the left and crossing the stubble where he'd already cut the corn.

Picking up the scythe, Joshua continued with the harvesting. He was thankful that Clara was safe, but wondered how much longer his own safety would be assured at the farmstead.

34

Joshua had almost finished reaping the first of the east fields when he heard Lizbet and Clara approach. The girl's voice was bright and cheerful as she joked about her newfound cleanliness thanks to falling into The Eddy. He turned and watched as they came along the path hand in hand, shaded by the boughs above as they passed through the strand of trees.

Clara set eyes on him and broke the bond with her mother, who was carrying a pail of water at her side. She ran to him with a wide smile, Joshua moving the scythe aside as she flung her arms about him, Rosie gripped in her right hand.

'My thanks,' she said breathlessly as she held him tight.

He looked to Lizbet, expectant of the girl being rebuked for her closeness, but seeing nothing but goodwill in her mother's expression. He let the scythe fall to the stubble and tentatively put his bound hands to Clara's back as she continued to embrace him.

'I owe you my life.'

'You owe me nothing,' he responded as Lizbet came to a halt a few yards away, still showing no sign of disapproval.

Clara looked up at him, her eyes shining. 'You done saved me and your actions will not soon be forgotten.'

'Your Ma be close on my heels and would've done saved you if I weren't there,' he said with genuine modesty.

'I fear I would have been too late,' said Lizbet.

'See,' said Clara with a grin, stepping back from him. 'Rosie thinks you be saving both our lives too.' She lifted the doll, its hair still damp. 'She thanks you also,' she added.

Joshua nodded, but still held with what he'd said, sure that Lizbet would have been in time to save her daughter's life. He bent to pick up the scythe.

'Wait!' called Lizbet, walking over to him.

'Hold out your hands,' she instructed after setting the pail of water on the stubble.

Joshua did as he was told and she reached for the binding about his wrists. She untied the bond and let it fall away, tucking the length of rope into her britches.

'Now it be easier to work,' she stated.

He gave another nod. 'Much obliged,' he said, resisting the urge to rub the rawness where the cord had abraded his skin, not wishing to be accused of making a show of his release.

He took up the scythe and held the two handles sticking out from its length, swinging the implement experimentally, the blade cutting the air. Turning to the remaining corn, he raised it and brought it across in front of him with a wide sweep, the ears tumbling.

'That be better,' he commented.

'Be you needing refreshment?' asked Clara, glancing at the pail.

Joshua shook his head. 'I'll be finishing with this field first,' he replied, setting to the task, his torso glistening with perspiration, the scars highlighted upon his back.

She looked away and her gaze settled on Bella. 'I'll go check her water,' she stated to her mother.

Lizbet nodded and watched as her daughter made her way over to the strip of grass between the field and trees, a thoughtful expression upon her face. She turned to look at Joshua, watching the scythe arc through the air and hearing the swish of the blade slicing through the stems. Her tongue was filled with the urge to offer her thanks, but she bit it back, reminding herself that he was only a nigger and was born to serve. He had done what was in him to do and no more.

She frowned, something within whispering of the vacuous nature of such thoughts. She had witnessed with her own eyes his concern and his eagerness to go to Clara's aid. There was more in it than mere servitude.

Lizbet shook her head, the battle between what had been instilled and what had been experienced continuing within her. She looked to the cut stems lying upon the field and tried to turn her attention to gathering.

She bent and began to collect a sheaf, glancing over to her daughter as she fussed Bella. Clara was in no doubt of the truth, but had little knowledge of the world.

'She be innocent of their nature,' she mumbled to herself, Joshua glancing over his shoulder, but making no enquiry.

Lizbet barely noticed the rot that darkened some of the ears as she worked, her mind turning to Clara's attachment to the negro. She worried that her daughter had not truly mourned the death of her Pa, but had replaced him to some degree with the runaway. This thought agitated her greatly. No nigger could possibly replace Walter and her daughter's inability to see this truth was like an affront to his memory.

Joshua finished cutting the last of the corn and turned to Lizbet. He watched a while as she snatched at the stems with obvious irritation. 'Done,' he stated, wiping his brow.

She glanced up, her gaze once more lacking kindness as she nodded her acknowledgement.

He walked over to the pail and crouched before it, cupping his hands and splashing his face before taking up some of the water in order to drink. Clara arose from where she was sitting on the grass and began to make her way over.

'Should I fetch some food?' she asked.

Lizbet didn't respond, her thoughts elsewhere as she grabbed at the corn.

'Ma?'

She looked over. 'What?'

'I be wondering if I should fetch some food?' reiterated Clara, seeing the look in her mother's eyes and feeling wary.

Lizbet nodded. 'While she gone, you can be starting on the other field,' she stated to Joshua before turning her attention back to gathering.

He glanced at Clara, who sought an answer as to her mother's change of mood, but found none in his expression. Taking up the scythe, the presence of blisters on his palms made plain after the brief respite, Joshua began towards the other field.

He passed over the weeds and grass between the pastures as Clara headed back to the cottage to fix a late lunch. The sun had already passed into the western sky and the shadows of the trees were beginning to draw out over the corn and stubble.

Joshua moved to the shaded corner of the field closest to the track that led back to the house. He readied himself, arms straining and blade at shoulder height before it swung down and cut the first stems. He worked without thought, drained by the heat and the labour, the rhythm of the work bringing the momentum by which to continue.

Clara soon returned bearing a tray draped with a cloth. She moved towards him, humming to herself as she did so, Joshua made glad that she was seemingly unaffected by her fright at the creek.

'As I done told you before, the negruh can wait,' stated Lizbet, straightening and putting her hands to her lower back as she winced.

Clara fell silent and her steps faltered. She looked regretfully at Joshua and then turned, making her way towards her mother as Lizbet plodded towards the shaded grass near the tethered cow.

Coming to a halt, she waited as her mother seated herself on the grass. Lizbet reached forward and pulled back the cloth to reveal three tin plates with slices of bread and pieces of cheese resting upon them.

'And water?' asked her mother.

'I thought we be drinking from the pail.'

'I ain't drinking that. The negruh's hands have been in it,' she stated, taking one of the plates. 'Go fetch us a cup each and leave the tray with me. He can continue until you're good and done.'

Clara frowned, her mother's hostility towards Joshua returned and with vigour. She put the tray on the grass and hurried back to the path, looking guiltily over at the slave as he watched her leave, their words having carried to him in the stillness.

'Get to your work, nigger,' instructed Lizbet, her treatment of him worsening as she battled with herself over his true nature.

He glanced at her and then returned his attention to the crop. The blade swung before him time and again as the crickets sounded and the shade in which he worked lengthened.

Catching movement in the corner of his eye, Joshua briefly looked over his shoulder to see Clara returning with a cup in each hand. She went to her mother and handed her one of the vessels before placing the other on the platter.

'Where are you going?' asked Lizbet as her daughter picked up the tray.

'To eat with Joshua.'

Lizbet shook her head. 'You be eating with me.'

'Then I be taking him his food.'

'What have I done said to you?' she asked. 'He can wait.'

Clara opened her mouth to protest, but saw the warning in her mother's eyes. She looked back at Joshua and then settled on the grass, covering the third plate so that flies could not settle and in the hope the bread would not stale before she took it to him.

'For what we are about to receive, may the Good Lord make us thankful. Amen.' Lizbet looked over at her daughter when she noted her failure to state the final word, a frown of disapproval upon her face, but making no comment.

Taking up her plate, Clara ate quickly, barely chewing the food before swallowing. There was a little soreness to her throat, a reminder of the incident that morning, one that in hindsight she thought would soften her mother towards Joshua.

She consumed the last piece of bread and took up her cup, following it down with a mouthful of water. 'I'm done,' she gasped, putting the cup and plate onto the tray.

Lizbet's frown deepened, only half her food as yet consumed.

'Can I be taking his plate over now?'

Her mother simply nodded her response, unable to think of any reason to delay her any longer.

Clara got up and then bent to take his plate. She walked out into the stubble and picked up the pail, arm straight at her side under its weight. She made her way over to him and Joshua stopped his reaping, turning to face her approach.

'You be earning this,' she said, holding the plate out to him.

'Much obliged,' he responded, setting the scythe on the ground before taking the food.

'Sit,' said Clara, lowering herself to the stubble between swathes of cut corn.

He followed suit, placing the bowl on his lap and thoughtfully looking across at her as he scratched his glistening beard. 'You should learn swimming before you be jumping in the crick,' he said with a forced smile as he lowered his hands, noting the tension in her expression that was caused by the expectation of her mother calling her back.

'Pa were going to learn me,' she replied, lowering her head and picking at a piece of straw. 'I miss him and in no small measure.'

Lizbet slowed her chewing as she listened to the words passing between her daughter and the runaway, keeping her gaze averted.

'It be no small loss,' responded Joshua with a nod, picking up the bread, its outermost dry to the touch.

'I can't be thinking about it for fear of falling into a lasting misery.'

'You loved him,' he stated, taking a bite, unable to resist the hunger that gnawed at him.

'I still do,' she replied, feeling the rise of tears. 'Ain't no words to describe it.'

'I be knowing that loss,' he said as he chewed.

Clara looked up at him with eyes glistening. 'What were your life like before you came upon the barn?' she asked, wishing to change the subject.

'Weren't no life,' he replied, taking another bite and not wanting to think back on his time at Benedict Farm.

They fell into silence as Joshua ate. Lizbet subtly looked over without raising her head, a poignant light in her eyes. Her daughter and the negro sat opposite each other in the shade, the corn as yet harvested standing beyond them and framing them in soft gold.

Something inside had given way upon hearing her daughter's admissions. The bonds that had enslaved her thoughts had come undone. She'd realised that Clara identified with the runaway's pain, felt its echo within her due to the loss of her father. He wasn't a replacement, merely a way to cope with the passing of her Pa.

Lizbet turned back to what was left of her food, her appetite gone as she felt guilty about how she'd spoken to her daughter earlier that day. She set her plate down upon the grass and took up her cup, drinking the water down. Standing, she looked about the field and then moved out into the stubble to continue with the gathering.

35

Clara knelt on the bank and washed her arms as Joshua stood in The Eddy. The light of day was all but gone, the late afternoon and evening spent transporting sheaves from South Field and the first of the east fields. They'd been placed in the empty stall where her father's horse had once been stabled and the work had only recently been halted, Lizbet leaving shortly before to wash up and prepare supper.

Clara began to hum to herself as the irritation left by the prick of straw began to lessen and she continued to cleanse her skin.

'Pull a stitch and I will mend,' sung Joshua, remembering the tune as if from some dream, his flight from dogs and men coming to mind.

'As sweet as molasses, as warm as the sun,

At my side when day is done.'

Clara smiled at him and they sung the second verse together, Joshua taking her lead if unsure of the next words.

'Rosie, oh Rosie, you're my best friend,

Side by side 'til the very end.

A Missouruh smile upon your face,

A belle of the south, make no mistake.'

Clara chuckled and smiled at him.

'A performance fit for any theatre,' said Joshua, clapping his hands. 'It may be we should tour the country.'

'We'd have to be taking her with us,' responded Clara, glancing at the doll tucked at her waist.

'Of course,' he nodded. 'A trio,' he added with a grin.

'I could arrive at more verses, maybe another song.'

Joshua nodded and then climbed out onto the bank, putting on his britches after running his hands down his legs to remove the excess water. 'I could learn me the fiddle and play along,' he said as he straightened, holding an imaginary fiddle and drawing the bow back and forth, doing a brief jig as he did so.

Clara laughed, the weight of the day's labour lifting from her.

'Supper be ready.'

They turned to her mother's call, Clara standing and seeing her on the porch. She waved in response and turned to Joshua in the half-light.

'Rabbit stew again, I'll warrant,' she commented with a roll of her eyes.

'A full belly be something to be thankful for, whatever be filling it,' he said as they began to walk from the mudflats.

They passed through the low gate, Clara sure to go first so as not to witness the disfigurement of his back. Moving to the porch, she stepped up and Joshua prepared to settle himself.

'The negruh can sit at the table,' stated Lizbet over her shoulder as she walked up the hallway opposite the front door.

Clara looked at her mother in puzzlement, watching her pass into the bedroom on the right. She glanced back at Joshua, who shrugged before following her into the cottage, a candle flickering at the centre of the table and the smell of rabbit stew hanging in the air.

Clara seated herself opposite the open shutters and Joshua took hold of the back of the chair nearest the door in order to pull it out.

'Joshua.'

He and Clara turned to find Lizbet returning to the room, expressions of surprise upon their faces after her use of his name. She stepped up to him, a folded shirt lying upon her palms.

'This be for you,' she stated, raising it slightly.

He glanced down and then looked to her eyes. 'You sure?'

Lizbet nodded. 'I only be sorry it weren't given sooner.'

Joshua took up the pale garment as Clara watched, a surge of love for her mother swelling her heart. The shirt bore the stains of previous labours in the fields and the cuffs were frayed, but its overall condition was sound.

Putting his arms through the sleeves, he buttoned the front and adjusted the collar. 'How do it look?' he asked, turning to the girl.

She nodded, unable to speak as she was overcome with emotion. She rose from her seat and went to Lizbet, hugging her close about the midriff.

'It were my husband's,' she stated as she stroked her daughter's hair, 'but suits you well.'

'I'm much obliged,' he responded with a nod. 'I ain't never been given such a fine gift before.' He looked down at the shirt admiringly.

There was a brief and awkward silence charged with words that went unsaid.

'Come, let us eat,' said Lizbet, motioning towards the table with one hand while gently ushering her daughter away with the other, feeling the threat of tears as a pang of loss came over her, the sight of the negro in Walter's shirt accentuating her husband's absence.

Clara returned to her seat, rendered speechless by her mother's treatment of Joshua and the feeling of adoration that arose in response. Joshua pulled out his intended chair and sat as Lizbet went to the stove, three bowls already resting on the cabinet beside.

Her back to the interior, she wiped tears from her eyes and then took up a ladle from beside the bowls. Taking each to the cooking pot, she filled them in turn and then took them to the table, spoons already in place. Fetching the breadboard that rested towards the rear of the cabinet, she placed it between them all, the candle flickering in the breath of her activity.

Sitting opposite her daughter, she looked across the table and found Clara staring at her with raw affection. The adoration in her daughter's eyes vanquished any lingering doubts as to her newfound hospitality towards the negro and she felt the prick of tears once again.

Swallowing against a tide of emotion, Lizbet placed her hands together. 'For what we are about to receive, may the Good Lord make us thankful,' she said with a weight of genuine feeling.

'Amen,' they all stated.

She smiled thinly across at her daughter and then turned to Joshua. 'Eat,' she instructed, nodding towards the steaming bowl placed before him and then taking up her spoon.

36

Joshua woke with a start. The water-muffled baying of hounds receded from his mind as the image of his body hanging from the submerged tree remained. The dream had come with more force than before and he considered the possibility that the fate it predicted was close at hand, that it was trying to stir him into action.

He stared at the vacancy beneath the eaves, the barn's interior faintly illuminated by the first light of day as he considered whether he should take flight. The smell of harvested corn filled his nose and he looked down between cracks in the boards, seeing the sheaves gathered in the stall beneath his position in the hayloft.

He glanced down his body, finding that he was wearing the shirt that Lizbet had given to him. He felt relieved that the kindness had not been just another dream and his tension abated a little.

Scrabbling arose from the hutches below and he wondered at the agitation of the rabbits. They were more lively than usual and, given the early hour, he was surprised that they were wakeful.

Lifting his torso, he tried to peer over the edge of the loft, wondering if a fox had managed to make its way into the building. Unable to see anything from his vantage point, Joshua crawled forward and went to the edge by the ladder.

Scanning the ground, he saw nothing of note within the relative darkness. The rabbits continued to cavort within their confinement and he looked to the cages.

'A rat?' he asked the stillness.

The recurring dream all but forgotten, he turned onto his back and rested his head on his hands, feeling the ache in his shoulders. He stared at the shingles above, pondering his fate once the harvest was gathered. All that remained was the rest of the second east field and a small pasture to the north.

He closed his eyes and considered whether Lizbet would reveal his presence once the corn had been cut and the sheaves gathered. Her treatment of him the night before had been but an aberration when held against their previous interactions. He judged it likely that she would return to her prior disdain and may even demand the return of her husband's shirt.

Joshua frowned and shook his head, berating himself for expending thought on the matter. It was wasted effort, only serving to compound his concerns and without any effect on what would actually come to pass.

His mind turned to Clara and his lips curled faintly upward as he recalled singing with her at the creek. A distant memory stirred in response. He remembered his mother singing to him on sleepless nights in the slave pen before he was taken from his parents. It had been a lullaby, its words accompanied by her arms wrapped warmly about him as he tried to find sleep.

Joshua tried to recall the first line. 'When time comes for the sun...,' he began, his expression becoming pinched as he sought the right words.

'When the sun goes to its bed,' he said with a nod of approval, the rest of the words being released by unlocking the opening line, ''tis time for you to rest your head, to seek out dreams and there to stay, 'til the dawn of a brand new day. Soft and light your dreams will be, the pillow of your liberty.

'Pillow, sweet pillow,' he sung, 'pillow of your liberty. Pillow, sweet pillow, where free you'll always be.'

Joshua sighed deeply, hearing the gentle melody of his mother's voice in the recesses of his memory. 'Pillow, sweet pillow,' he said to himself, a tear rolling down his cheek and the world caught in the impermanence of its reflections.

37

'There be a strap of leather hanging in the barn for sharpening,' stated Lizbet as she collected the bowls from the table, piling them atop each other.

Joshua nodded and pushed back his seat. He had found that her kinder disposition had not fled during the night. She had invited him to join them to break the fast, the invitation coming via her daughter. The three of them had spoken little as they ate bowls of oatmeal, fuel taken ahead of the locomotion of labour.

'Clara, you be washing the cups and bowls at The Eddy, and mind how you go. We ain't wanting a repeat of yesterday's commotion.'

'I can second that,' she responded, finishing her water and then getting off her chair.

'You want I should head out to the east fields when I've done sharpened the blade?' asked Joshua as Clara placed the cups on top of each other and then into the uppermost bowl.

Lizbet nodded. 'I'll be joining you when I'm done here.'

The small tower of cups threatened to topple as Clara lifted the pile from the tabletop. She tried to correct with over-enthusiasm and the top cup fell.

Joshua stooped and caught it just before it hit the ground, smiling as he straightened and held it out to her.

'It seems you be a saviour,' observed Lizbet, 'what with the timely harvesting and my daughter's life already owed to you.'

'I just be in the right place when needed,' he responded, 'and glad for it.'

He walked to the doorway and stepped out onto the porch.

'Joshua,' called Lizbet.

He paused and looked back at her as she stood by the table.

'You have my gratitude.'

He nodded and then continued on, taking the path to the barn.

Clara looked at her mother as she gauged her words. 'You seem to be of different mind in regards his presence.'

'I am of different mind in regards him, but not his presence,' she corrected. 'He cannot be staying here, Clara. The risk to us be too great.'

'If you be seeing he's done saved us from a lean winter and that he done saved my life, then surely you can see he has earned his place here.'

'He has earned his place at our table while he abides on the farm, but his residence cannot be granted,' replied Lizbet, walking around to crouch in front of her daughter and holding her gaze. 'He be the property of another.'

'Then let us buy him.'

'We have little left bar that set aside for hard times,' she stated, placing her hand on her daughter's shoulder. 'Even if we had a fair fortune, his Master may not wish to sell or to be left unsatisfied when it comes to punishment for his running away.'

'Can't we try?'

Lizbet shook her head. 'It would not be enough, Clara. I don't say so with pleasure, for I have seen the truth of the man. You saw it from the outset and I'm sorry I didn't see it sooner.' She gave her daughter's shoulder a squeeze. 'It would seem the eyes of a child see with

188

greater clarity than an adult at times,' she added with a thin smile.

Clara's expression remained downcast. She could think of no other argument by which to persuade her mother to keep Joshua at the farm.

'Now, be taking the dirty bowls to the crick and don't be falling in,' she said, stroking Clara's cheek before straightening. 'When you're done, the rabbits are in want of feed and the chickens can be let into South Field so as to pick the fallen grains.'

Clara stood motionless, still searching for some way by which Joshua could remain with them.

'Run along,' instructed her mother, gently pushing her towards the door, 'and when all's done you can bring us out a pail of water for refreshment and stay for awhile before attending to the sweeping.'

Clara's mood wasn't improved by her concession, by the prospect of spending time with them in the east fields. She walked sullenly to the door and passed out of the cottage, stepping off the porch and glancing to the east before heading in the opposite direction.

Her shoulders sagged as she carried the pile of bowls and cups in both hands, nudging open the gate with her knee and passing through. Keeping a wary eye on the thick grasses to either side of the track, she made her way to the mudflats.

She scanned them for any sign of a snake as she made her way to the water's edge. Remaining alert to any danger, she set the bowls down beside her and then knelt before The Eddy.

Clara lifted out the cups and put them aside. She commenced with cleaning each bowl in turn, her mind occupied with thoughts of her mother's unshakeable intention to visit with Tyler and tell him of Joshua's presence. She piled the bowls upon her lap, ignoring the faint dampness seeping through her faded yellow dress.

Taking up the first cup, she suddenly turned to her right, eyes wide and fearful. Her gaze settled on the bowed and swaying head of grass that had seemed to her like the movement of a snake when seen from the corner of her eye. She frowned at it and scanned the undergrowth where it gave way to the mud, seeing nothing of concern.

Finishing the task, she held the bottom bowl and carefully stood, staring intently at the top cup as if forcing it to remain in place by will alone. She turned towards the cottage and squinted, the low sun shining brightly through the tops of the trees beyond the barn.

She narrowed her eyes further as she walked from the flats, her movement creating a flickering and golden interference in the field of her vision. Passing through the gate, she bowed her head to avoid the continuing flash of sunbeams.

The whinny of a horse and thud of numerous hooves brought Clara's gaze upward once again. She looked to the gap between the house and barn, the sounds seeming to emanate from behind the cottage. Stopping by the porch, a mixture of nervousness and curiosity kept her steadfast as the horses drew closer.

38

Joshua lifted the scythe and went still, brow furrowing as he detected a sound of approach. He glanced over his shoulder to see Lizbet moving into the field from the path.

Nodding his acknowledgement of her arrival, he turned back and the blade swept down. He continued to harvest the corn as she went to the fallen stems in his wake, readying herself to gather.

Lizbet stared at the cut corn for a moment and then looked to his back, his scars hidden by Walter's shirt. 'You know you can't be staying,' she stated, regret in her tone.

'I knows it,' he replied without faltering in his work.

'I wish it weren't so but...' The sentence failed in her throat, guilt and shame stealing her words. She knew it was but self-preservation that motivated the need to reveal his presence at the farm, but also knew there were few that would conduct matters in any other way.

Joshua made no response, but continued in his task. He understood there was little choice open to her, that both hers and Clara's lives would be at risk should they secret him away on the farm. He wished it weren't so also, but neither wishes nor prayers had ever been granted him.

The whinny of a horse and sound of hooves drew his gaze towards the trees that masked the buildings of the farmstead. He lowered the head of the scythe to the ground with a look of curiosity upon his glistening face.

'Your Master?' asked Lizbet with concern.

Joshua turned to her, his expression tightening with fear.

She broke into a low stride, making her way toward the strand of trees. He watched a moment, his heart pounding and the strength of the recurring ream recalled. Forcing his legs into motion, he then followed her to the shadowed undergrowth.

They crept through the thin woodland and tried to find a clear line of sight that would allow a view of the barn and cottage beyond. Lizbet neared the western edge of the strand, crouching behind a bush as she spied Clara standing by the porch staring at the passage between the buildings. Joshua moved to her side, the pair of them barely daring to take a breath as they waited for the riders to come into view.

A dozen men rode into sight to the squawks of scattering chickens. They were a ragtag band, their appearance dishevelled and dusty. Pistols were holstered at their hips and they carried rifles across their laps in readiness.

Lizbet's eyes widened and she was struck with sudden nausea when she spied the reddish-brown leggings tied about their shins.

'Jayhawkers,' she whispered, swallowing back the sickness, 'fighting for the Union.'

'Howdy,' said the lead horseman, holstering his rifle and touching the brim of his hat as he brought his steed to a halt before Clara, the girl looking small and vulnerable before the riders.

She nodded her response, her gaze restless as the other men pulled up and looked about the buildings and South Field. 'Be you from Benedict Farm?' she asked, worried that they'd come looking for Joshua.

The leader looked to the other man with a knowing smile as he briefly lifted his hat to wipe sweat from his brow. 'You could be saying we was, in a roundabout kinda way,' he answered, his men chuckling.

Joshua looked at Lizbet in shock, his mouth hanging open. She nodded, confirming his estimation of the man's meaning.

'Where be your Ma and Pa?'

'My Pa died fighting for the Confederacy,' she responded, ignorant of the allegiance of the irregular soldiers arrayed before her.

'Did he now?' grinned the captain, glancing around at his men again, a couple of them snorting in response. 'Then that be one less traitor we have need of putting to the sword.'

Clara's expression dropped as realisation dawned. Lizbet went to rise and Joshua grabbed her arm tightly, pulling her back down into their concealment.

He shook his head. 'Reveal yourself and we all be dead,' he whispered.

'And your Ma?' asked the captain, scratching his dark beard.

'She be...' Clara looked at the men's faces. 'She be not here.'

'Ruskin, Carver, check the barn,' he ordered, glancing over at the building.

'That be a fine doll you got there,' he commented, a lopsided smile upon his rugged face. 'Can I be taking a closer look?' He held out his hand.

'I must go to her,' said Lizbet, her eyes pleading with Joshua to release her.

He shook his head as they remained hidden and two of the soldiers rode to the barn, dismounting and going inside. 'There be nothing you can do,' he responded, his grip unrelenting.

Clara put the bowls and cups down on the porch step, never taking her gaze from the captain. She took Rosie from her waist and clasped the doll to her chest, shaking her head weakly.

'Come now, I ain't gonna to do her no harm.'

She looked to the other men. They watched her intently and one moved his hand to the gun holstered at his hip as her gaze briefly rested upon him.

With hand trembling, she held Rosie out towards the leader, her heart racing and feeling faint.

'You'll have to step closer,' stated the captain, his eyes gleaming malevolently within the shadow cast by the brim of his hat.

'Run, Clara. Run,' whispered Lizbet, tears in her eyes as her daughter took a hesitant step towards the captain.

He nudged his horse in the flanks and it stepped forward. Reaching down, he made to take the doll and quickly grasped her wrist. Clara let out a yell and yanked her hand back, releasing Rosie in fright. Her slender fingers slipped from his hold and she turned for the shelter of the house.

Lizbet tried to rise again, but Joshua held her in place as they watched Clara run into the cottage, flinging the door shut behind her. The two soldiers that had been sent into the barn exited and shook their heads when the captain looked over.

'She ain't in there, but we found us something for supper,' said Ruskin, holding up a brace of rabbits, his face grimy and his lank hair topped by a stovepipe hat.

'Seems as though you won't be sowing no wild oats this time, boys,' responded the captain with a grin.

'You want we should torch it?' asked Carver as Ruskin tucked one of the creatures beneath his arm and gripped the other in both hands, Lizbet wincing as he broke its neck, sure that it was Elsa.

'Raise it to the ground,' nodded the captain. 'Pitt, McCawley, head round the back and set a fire. Keep an eye out for the girl.'

Two of the riders passed back around the side of the house and out of view. The men who had checked the barn took cans from their steeds and dowsed the sides of the building with oil, the captain taking another from where it hung behind his right leg. He encouraged his horse forward and emptied some of the contents over the porch and front of the house.

Moving back a few yards, he took some tobacco and papers from a pocket in his dark jacket. With disturbing calmness, he rolled a cigarette, licking the paper and sealing it before placing it to his lips. Producing a match, he struck it against the rough pommel of his saddle.

The head failed to light and he repeated the process. The match flared and the sulphurous light was reflected in his shadowed eyes. Cupping his free hand to protect the flame, he lit the cigarette and took a long drag, holding the burning match for what seemed like an eternity.

He nonchalantly flicked it towards the cottage. It arced through the air, the flame fading and seeming as if it would fail, as if Lizbet and Joshua's prayers would be answered as they watched from the trees.

It landed on the porch and the oil took in a rush of eager consumption. Smoke began to rise from the rear of the cottage as another fire took hold.

'You got a match going spare, Captain?' called Ruskin from beside the barn.

He sighed with dissatisfaction and rode over to the building, taking another from his pocket as he did so. 'Watch those tail feathers, boys,' he stated, striking it and immediately flicking it to the slats as Ruskin and Carver ran to a safe distance.

The wall flared and the flames began to lick upward. Those consuming the cottage grew stronger, reaching into the main room and up the roof with surprising speed as dark smoke poured into the sky.

High screams began to arise from within.

'Clara!' exclaimed Lizbet breathlessly, the sound of the fires masking her soft cry.

She and Joshua watched helplessly as the captain returned to his previous position in front of the cottage, leisurely smoking his cigarette as Clara's screams continued to lift with the fumes of the fires that were rapidly devouring the cottage.

The cries of terror fell silent and Lizbet began to weep, falling against Joshua. He placed his arms about her and felt the jolting of her misery, his own eyes swollen with tears as he continued to watch.

The captain finished smoking the cigarette, flicking the butt towards the house as part of the roof collapsed to the rear, timbers splintering and embers rising into the morning sky. 'Our work be done here, boys,' he said, taking up the reins and turning to his men. 'We head south.'

He led them off, moving across South Field to join the track before the southern strand of trees. More of the cottage's roof fell into charred ruin as the Union irregulars passed out of sight, the sound of hooves diminishing in their wake.

Joshua and Lizbet remained hidden. She sobbed against his shoulder and he turned his gaze from the roaring fires that consumed the buildings with haste, the air above rippling as towers of smoke rose to the sky. He held her, both giving and drawing what little comfort was afforded by the embrace.

They stayed in their concealment for a long time, their misery accompanied by sounds of consumption and collapse. As the flames lost their vigour, their fuel all but spent, Lizbet pulled away from him and stood. She stared at the wreckage of the house, the stone-built chimney stack rising as testament to what had been so recently her home.

'Clara,' she whispered, pushing through the undergrowth, dazed and lost to her sorrow.

Joshua followed behind, the smell of smoke heavy in his nostrils as they passed the remains of the barn, the chicken coop unscathed on the opposite side of the path. His legs were heavy, body with a greater weight than any he'd known before.

Lizbet knelt before the cottage and he watched as she picked something up from the ground. She turned to him and he saw Rosie within her grasp, her glistening eyes filled with the pain of her loss.

'Rosie, oh Rosie,' she said softly, tears beginning to stream down her cheeks as she looked back to the doll and began to stroke its red hair.

'Ma?'

Joshua looked to the ruins with wide eyes and pulse racing. Lizbet turned her gaze heavenward, confusion mingling with her sadness.

'Ma?' The word was followed by coughing.

Joshua moved forward into the devastation. 'Clara?'

More coughing arose, an echoing quality to its rasp.

He stared at the large chimney and saw a pail placed at its entrance. Making his way over as Lizbet rose to her feet, he saw the last hint of water within the bucket and then noted the blackened and blistered feet beyond.

He moved the pail aside with haste, the metal still hot to the touch. 'Clara,' he stated, crouching and setting eyes on her as she cowered to the rear.

Joshua held his arms out to her and she began to cry as she went to him and fell into his embrace, coughing against his shoulder. He lifted her, his own tears falling as he held her with the tightness of relief.

Lizbet stared in disbelief as he walked from the smouldering ruin with her blackened daughter in his arms. 'Clara?' she whispered, barely daring to say her name for fear the illusion of her survival would be broken.

Clara turned, the soot upon her face streaked by the passage of tears. 'Ma,' she said hoarsely, having to clear her throat, the fumes that had escaped up the chimney leaving a residue of irritation.

Lizbet stepped up to them and Joshua passed her daughter into her eager arms. She looked down at her face, seeing the evidence of mild burns beneath the stain of fumes. 'I thought I'd lost you.'

Clara shook her head.

'It be a miracle,' commented Joshua, mother and daughter turning to him.

There was a moment of contemplative silence.

'You can stay now, can't he, Ma?' said Clara, looking back to her mother and coughing briefly.

'Yes,' she replied, turning her gaze to Joshua. 'You can stay, if you that be your choice now your freedom has come.'

'I'll be staying,' he confirmed with a nod.

Clara weakly reached out to him and he took her hand, holding it firmly.

'Don't fret, Ma, we can build it again,' she said, noting her mother's glance towards the wreckage of the cottage, 'and this time there'll be three bedrooms.'

Lizbet looked to her daughter to find her grinning as she lay cradled in her arms. She nodded. 'This time there'll be three bedrooms,' she confirmed before drawing Clara to her chest and holding her close.

Epilogue

Lizbet rode between the trees, her misted breath hanging in the winter stillness. The horse beneath her had been found wandering after Tyler's farm had suffered the same fate as her own not more than half a day later. The cart behind had been salvaged from the ruins and Tyler's body buried.

South Field came into view, its ploughed furrows thick with snow broken by ridges of soil between. The cottage lay beyond, its fresh timbers beginning to show signs of weathering as the months wore on. She had been gone eight days and its sight was a joy to behold, a smile dawning upon her face as the cart creaked and rocked through hidden ruts.

The door opened and Clara came into view wearing woollen leggings with Rosie tucked into the top, her boots loose after having been put on in haste in response to the sound of her mother's approach. She rushed from the porch and cut across the field rather than following the track to the left, stumbling through the furrows.

Joshua stepped into the doorway, his feet bare as he watched the girl make haste towards her mother. Lizbet reached down as her daughter neared and then heaved her up, Clara settling in front of her.

'How were St Louis? Did you buy more rabbits?' she asked, looking over her shoulder.

'Next time,' responded Lizbet, looking forward to enjoying the heat of the fire, a pennant of smoke rising from the chimney which Walter had built. She looked to it, knowing that in its existence her husband lived on. His body may have passed, but the consequence of his life upon the world remained and had saved their daughter's life.

'You didn't get any?' There was disappointment in Clara's tone.

Her mother shook her head as the horse moved around the corner of the field.

'What did you buy, then?' she enquired, trying to peer round her mother to the contents of the cart.

Joshua watched as the horse drew close. Lizbet looked at him meaningfully and his pulse became elevated as she communicated something without need of words, glancing back over her shoulder.

His gaze went to the cart as she drew the horse to a stop alongside the porch. A figure sat hunched within, a hood pulled over their head.

He moved out of the doorway on weakened legs, body trembling with the force of his heartbeat as he stepped to the snow that lay upon the ground. Walking to the rear, he stared unblinking at the figure seated before him.

They lifted their hands and drew back the hood. A black woman with greying hair was revealed and their eyes met. They were eyes he had never forgotten, never could forget.

'Ma?'

She struggled to rise and stepped to the rear. He stared up at her, his expression one of shocked wonder.

'Joshua,' she stated, her warm words wrapping about him and tightening his chest.

He raised his hand without thought, his mind unable to bring forth words. Helping her down, he still found himself unable to take his gaze from her.

She stood before him, smaller than he remembered and the years since their enforced parting etched upon her face, the wrinkles that had only been soft creases about her eyes now deep.

'She has her freedom, thanks to Lincoln and the Union,' commented Lizbet.

In sudden movement, he took her into his arms and they embraced as Clara and Lizbet looked on with smiles upon their faces.

'Joshua,' she whispered into his ear. 'We both have our freedom now. Ain't no need for a pillow to find it no more.'

He wept with abandon, collapsing into her presence as the snow began to fall, soft and silent as it settled upon them and caressed their skin with immaculate lips.

Afterward

After writing *The Hanging Tree* I was acutely aware that many readers of that tale would be left feeling melancholic. Because of this I wanted to write another story relating to slavery which would be positive and uplifting in order to create a balance with the tragic tone of *The Hanging Tree*. The inspiration for *Runaway* arose quite naturally from this desire and did not need to be forced in any way.

I wrote *Runaway* in four weeks and a day, most days the writing being done early in the mornings, which was a change compared with the past, when much of my work had been conducted in the evenings and late at night. The simplicity of the plot and minimal amount of main characters leant itself well to an intimate story in which the nuances of the tale could be played out.

As usual, I did not force the story along any particular route. I had one in mind, but did not stick to it rigidly or make the characters follow it when I could feel that they wanted to deviate. They took on a life of their own and acted out of their natures, sometimes taking the story in unexpected directions. For instance, I had no idea that Lizbet would venture to St Louis for rabbits at the end and certainly did not expect her to return instead with Joshua's mother. I also didn't anticipate the 'Sweet Pillow' song, nor how it would resonate when mother and son were reunited.

I hope this story has resonated with you and moved you in a positive manner. For those of you interested in the historical background of this tale, there are a few facts to follow. Thank you for reading my work and may you have liberty in regards both your body and your mind.

Historical Elements Relevant to the Story:

1. President Lincoln made his Emancipation Proclamation on the 22nd September 1862. This proclamation declared all slaves 'forever free' and took effect on the 1st January 1863. However, as the Civil War neared its end, Lincoln was concerned about the legality of the proclamation once fighting ceased and so pushed for the 13th Amendment to the Constitution to be passed by Congress. This amendment concerned the abolition of slavery and was passed on the 31st January 1865, shortly before hostilities between the Union and Confederacy came to an end. It was later ratified on the 6th December in the same year.

2. Disease had a large part to play in the American Civil War. It caused two-thirds of combatant mortality and also greatly effected civilians. Over 80,000 Union soldiers died from typhoid or dysentery, which is considerably more than died from battle wounds. Malaria and yellow fever also contributed to the mortality rate.

3. During the early part of the Civil War bands of guerrilla fighters from Missouri would cross the border into Kansas and carry out attacks. They were known as 'Border Ruffians' and Union irregulars termed 'Jawhawkers' were banded together in order to combat these Confederate incursions. The term 'Jayhawker' did not become synonymous with people from Kansas until after the war.

4. Missouri was a divided state during the war. Men, armies, generals and supplies were sent to both sides. There were two competing state governing bodies, one for the Union and one for the Confederacy. Both sides claimed the state as theirs and its star was shown on both flags. Representatives were sent to the United States Congress and the Confederate Congress. This created great division within the state, neighbour pitted against neighbour, and an intrastate war effectively took place within the context of the greater conflict.

5. There were a number of slave pens located in St Louis, including one that 'specialised' in the sale of children. One of the best known was Lynch's Slave Pen. When Union forces took over on 3rd September 1861, it was turned into a prison for Confederate sympathisers, Lynch himself leaving the city in order to join the Confederacy.

On a final note, 20% of the proceeds from *Runaway* will be donated to the charity Anti-Slavery International. The U.K. abolished slavery in 1833 and the U.S. in 1865, but its blight is still present in the world today with an estimated 21 million people living under its yoke, visit www.antislavery.org to find out more. On behalf of all those who you will be helping by buying this book, thank you.

If you enjoyed *Runaway* then try the novella *The Hanging Tree*, which tells the story of two slaves in love on a Louisiana plantation.

Alternatively, try the series of three historical novels set in the far south-west of England. Called *Where Seagulls Fly* (2013 Edition), *Song of the Sea* and *The Shepherd of St Just*, each tells the tale of an outcast.

For a contemporary story that is sure to keep you gripped and which has the underlying theme of our interconnectedness, try *Quiddity* (2013 Edition).

All the above are available in paperback and Kindle formats and are among the many books written by Edwin Page.

Printed in Great Britain
by Amazon